OUTW...

JOHN ... ...
LUCAS PARKES

PENGUIN BOOKS

IN ASSOCIATION WITH
MICHAEL JOSEPH

Penguin Books Ltd, Harmondsworth, Middlesex, England
Penguin Books Australia Ltd, Ringwood, Victoria, Australia

—

Chapters 1 to 4 first published by Michael Joseph 1959
Published with Chapter 5 by Science Fiction Book Club 1961
Published in Penguin Books 1962
Reprinted 1964, 1967, 1970, 1971, 1973

—

Copyright © the Estate of John Wyndham, and Lucas Parkes, 1959

—

Made and printed in Great Britain
by C. Nicholls & Company Ltd
Set in Linotype Pilgrim

This book is sold subject to the condition
that it shall not, by way of trade or otherwise,
be lent, re-sold, hired out, or otherwise circulated
without the publisher's prior consent in any form of
binding or cover other than that in which it is
published and without a similar condition
including this condition being imposed
on the subsequent purchaser

CONTENTS

ONE   *The Space-Station:* A.D. 1994   9

TWO   *The Moon:* A.D. 2044   44

THREE *Mars:* A.D. 2094   94

FOUR *Venus:* A.D. 2144   130

FIVE *The Emptiness of Space:*
      THE ASTEROIDS A.D. 2194   169

THE TROON LINE

George Montgomery Troon – Laura
(*On the space-station construction*)

George Michael Troon (b. 1994)
(*Commander British Moon Station*)

Son (b. 2016)　　　　Son (b. 2019)
(*Emigrated to Brazil. Changed name to Trunho*)

Son (b. 2038)

Geoffrey Montgomery Trunho (b. 2066) – Isabella
(*First Mars landing*)

George Trunho (b. 2091)　　　Geof. Michael Trunho (b. 2094)　　　Geo. Montgomery Troon (b. 2117) – D. Filey
　　　　　　　　　　　　　　　　(*Became Australian citizen. Widow*　　(*First successful Venus landing*)
　　　　　　　　　　　　　　　　restored surname to Troon)

Anna – H.P. Gonveia　　Jorge Manoel Trunho
(b. 2088)　　　　　　　(b. 2120)

Jayme A. Gonveia
(b. 2118)

ONE

THE SPACE-STATION

A.D. 1994

TICKER TROON emerged from his final interview filled with an emulsion of astonishment, elation, respect, and conviction that he needed refreshment.

The interview had begun formally, as he had expected. Announced by the clerk, he had marched in smartly, and come to attention before the wide desk. The old boy behind it had turned out to be a considerably older boy than he had been prepared for, but his type was authentic. Lean, he was, with a handsome, slightly weathered, aristocratic face, carefully trimmed hair that was quite white, and rows of ribbons on his left breast.

He had raised his eyes from a clipful of forms to inspect his visitor carefully, and even at that point Ticker had begun to have a suspicion that the interview was not going to be entirely routine, for the old boy – or, to identify him more fully, Air Marshal Sir Godfrey Wilde – did not employ simply that keen-eyed air of summing one's man up at leisure and appearing incompletely satisfied, which had been the drill at lower grades of interviews. He was really looking at Ticker as a person, and somewhat oddly, too. Still looking, he nodded slowly to himself two or three times.

'Troon,' he said, reflectively. 'Flight-Lieutenant George Montgomery Troon. Very probably known in some circles, I suspect, as Ticker Troon?'

Ticker had been startled.

'Er – yes, sir.'

The old boy smiled a little. 'The young are seldom very

original. G. M. Troon – G. M. T. – hence, deviously, Ticker.'

He had gone on regarding Ticker steadily, with a length of inspection that passed the bounds of custom, and of comfort. Ticker grew embarrassed, and had to resist the temptation to shift uneasily. The old boy became aware of the awkwardness. His face relaxed into a smile that was friendly, and reassuring.

'Forgive me, my boy. I was fifty years away,' he said.

He glanced down at the forms. Ticker recognized some of them. His whole history was there. Troon, G. M., aged twenty-four, single, C. of E. Parentage ... education ... service details ... medical report ... C.O.'s report ... security report, no doubt ... probably a private-life report ... notes on friends, and so on, and so on ... Quite a bundle of stuff, altogether. The old boy evidently thought so too, for he pushed it all aside with a touch of impatience, waved his hand at an easy chair, and slid over a silver cigarette-box.

'Sit down there, my boy,' he invited.

'Thank you, sir,' Ticker had said. And he had taken the offered cigarette, doing his best to give an impression of ease.

'Tell me,' said the old boy, in a friendly tone, 'what made you apply for transfer from Air to Space?'

It was an expected, standard question, to which there was a standard answer, but it was not put in the standard way, and, with the man's eye thoughtfully upon him, Ticker decided against giving the standard reply. He frowned, a little uncertainly.

'It isn't easy to explain, sir. In fact, I'm not honestly sure that I know. It – well, it isn't that I *had* to do it. But there is a kind of inevitable feeling about it – as if it were a thing I was bound to do, sooner or later. My natural next step ...'

'*Next* step,' repeated the Air Marshal. 'Not your crowning ambition, then? Next step towards what?'

The Space-Station

'I don't really know, sir. Outwards, I think. There's a sort of sense I can't explain ... a kind of urge onwards and outwards. It is not a sudden idea, sir. It seems always to have been there, at the back of my mind. I'm afraid it all sounds a bit vague. . . . ' He let himself trail off, inadequately.

But the old boy did not seem to find it inadequate. He gave a couple of his slow nods, and leant back in his chair. For a few moments he gazed up at the cornice of the ceiling, seeming to search his memory. Presently, he said:

> '... for all the night
> I heard their thin gnat-voices cry
> Star to faint star across the sky.'

He brought his gaze down to Ticker's surprised face.

'That mean anything to you?' he asked.

Hesitantly, Ticker said:

'I think so, sir. Where does it come from?'

'I was told it was Rupert Brooke – though I've never found the context. But the man I first heard it from was your grandfather.'

'My – my grandfather, sir?' Ticker stared.

'Yes. The other George Montgomery Troon – and does it surprise you to know that he was Ticker Troon, too? Grandfather!' He shook his head, ruefully. 'It always seems to be a word for old fellows like me. But Ticker – well, he never had the chance. He was dead, you know, before he was your age.'

'Yes, sir. Did you know him well?'

'I did indeed. We were in the same squadron when it happened. You look amazingly like him. I was expecting you, of course; nevertheless, it gave me quite a shock when you came in.' The Air Marshal had paused at that, somewhat lengthily. Then he went on: 'He had that feeling, too. He flew because that was as far *outwards* as we could get

The Outward Urge

in those days – as far as most of us ever expected to get. But not Ticker. I can remember even now the way he used to look up at the night sky, at the moon and the stars, and talk about them as if it were a foregone conclusion that we'd be going out there some day – and sadly, too, because he knew that he'd never be going out there himself. We used to think it comic-strip stuff in those days, but he'd smile off the ragging and the arguments as if he just *knew*.' There had been another long pause then before he added: 'God, I'm sorry old Ticker can't know about this. If there's one thing that'd make him as pleased as Punch, it'd be to know that his grandson wants to go "out there".'

'Thank you, sir. It's good to know that,' Ticker had told him. And then, feeling that the ball had been passed to him, he added: 'He was killed over Germany, wasn't he, sir?'

'Berlin. August 1944,' said the Air Marshal. 'A big op. His aircraft blew up.' He sighed, reminiscently. 'When we got back, I went to see his wife, your grandmother. She was a lovely girl, a sweet girl. She took it hard. She went away somewhere, and I lost touch with her. She is still alive?'

'Very much so, sir. She married again in, I think, 1949.'

'I'm glad of that. Poor girl. They were only married a week before he was killed, you know.'

'Only a week, sir. I didn't know it was as short as that.'

'It was. So your father, and consequently yourself, may be said to exist at all, only by a very narrow margin. They had married a little earlier than they intended. Perhaps Ticker had a premonition: most of us did, though some of us were wrong.'

There was another pause which lasted until the Air Marshal roused himself from his thoughts to say:

'You have stated here that you are single.'

'Yes, sir,' agreed Ticker.

He became abruptly conscious of the special licence in

The Space-Station

his pocket, and all but looked down to see if it were protruding.

'That was a condition of application, of course,' said the old man. 'Are you, in fact, unmarried?'

'Yes, sir,' Ticker said again, with an uneasy feeling that the pocket might have become transparent.

'And you have no brother?'

'No, sir.'

The Air Marshal remarked, consideringly:

'The stated purpose of this qualification is at variance with my experience. I have never found in war that the married officer is less redoubtable than the single man: rather the other way, in fact. One is led to suspect, therefore, that the matter of pensions and subsequent responsibilities is allowed inappropriate weight. Would you say that it is a good principle that our fittest young men should not infrequently be dissuaded from procreation while the less fit retain the liberty to breed like rabbits?'

'Er – no, sir,' Ticker said, wonderingly.

'Good,' said the Air Marshal. 'I am very glad to hear it.'

He maintained such a steady regard that Ticker was all but impelled to confess the presence of the licence. Prudence, however, still kept a fingertip hold on him. When the old boy had spoken again, it was to turn the interview on to more conventional lines.

'You understand the need for top security in this work?' he inquired.

Ticker felt easier.

'Security has been very much stressed all along, sir.'

'But you don't know why?'

'I've been given no details, sir.'

'Nevertheless, as an intelligent young man you must have formed some ideas.'

'Well, sir, from what I have heard and read about

13

The Outward Urge

experimental space missiles, I should think the time can't be far off now when we shall start to build some kind of space-station – possibly a manned satellite. Would it be something of that sort?'

'It would indeed, my boy – though your deductions are not quite up to date, I'm glad to say. The space-station already exists – in parts. And some of the parts are already up there. Your job will be to help in the assembly.'

Ticker's eyes widened, lit up with enthusiasm.

'I say, sir, that's wonderful. I'd no idea ... I thought we were rather behind in this sort of thing. Assembling the first space-station ...!' He trailed off, incoherently.

'I did not say it was the first,' the old man reminded him. 'In fact, there *may* be others.'

Ticker looked shocked. The Air Marshal amplified:

'It doesn't do to take things for granted. After all, we know that the Americans, and the Other Fellows, too, have been working hard on it – and our resources are nothing like theirs.'

Ticker stared.

'I thought we'd be working *with* the Americans, sir.'

'So we ought to be. We're certainly not working against them, but it just so happens that our people remember *their* love of public announcements at politically happy moments; and *they* remember certain leaks in our security system. Result: we go our different ways – with a great waste of time and energy in duplication of work. On the other hand, it will allow us to stand on our own feet in space – if that expression may be permitted – instead of being taken along as poor relations. That might one day turn out to have its advantages.'

'I suppose so, sir. And the Other Fellows ...?'

'Oh, they're at work on it, all right. They were known to be working on an unmanned satellite forty years ago

The Space-Station

when the Americans stole their thunder by making the first public announcement on satellites. But they got their own back by putting the first one into orbit. Just how far they've got now is a matter on which this Department would like a lot more information than it has.

'Now, as to yourself: first of all there'll be conditioning and training....'

Ticker's thoughts were far too chaotic for him to give proper attention to the details that followed. He was looking beyond the walls of the sunlit office and already seeing the fire-pointed blackness of space. In imagination he could feel himself floating in the void. In a – abruptly he became aware that the Air Marshal had ceased to talk, and was looking at him as if after a question. He tried to pull himself together.

'I'm awfully sorry, sir. I didn't quite follow ...'

'I can see I'm wasting my time now,' the old man had said, but without rancour. Indeed, he had smiled. 'I've seen that look before. I think you'll do. But perhaps one day you'll be good enough to explain to me why a Troon is habitually thrown into a form of hypnotic trance at the thought of space.' He rose. Ticker jumped up, quickly. 'Remember the security – this is *top* secret. The kind of thing you would not let even your wife guess – if, of course, you were so fortunate as to have one. You appreciate that?'

'I do, sir.'

'Good-bye, then – er – Ticker. And good luck.'

Ticker had thanked him in a not quite steady voice.

Afterwards, in the first convenient saloon-bar, with a whisky in front of him, he pulled the special marriage licence out of his pocket, and considered it again. He wished now that he had not been so carried away; that he had

15

The Outward Urge

listened with more care to what the old boy had been telling him. Something about a conditioning course of twelve weeks, and studying the space-station, both in plan and mock-up. And something about a bit of leave, too. Could that be right? After all, if they had some of the sections up there already, wouldn't they be about finished by the time he was trained and ready to go? He 'was momentarily alarmed – until his common sense asserted itself: you couldn't just throw the pieces of a space-station up into the sky and let them come together. Every part must be ferried there, laboriously, monotonously, very, very expensively, and in quite small bits at a time. It would be far and away the most costly structure ever built. There would have to be heaven knew how many journeys up there before they had enough to start on the assembly. Thinking of only that aspect of the problem caused him to swing gloomily to the other extreme – why, it was more likely to take years and years before it could be fully assembled and in working order. . . .

He dredged around in his mind for what the old boy had said about spells of duty: four weeks on, four weeks off – though that was hypothetical at present, and might need modification in the light of experience. All the same, the intention sounded generous enough, not bad at all. . . .

He returned his attention to the marriage licence in his hand. There could be no doubt that from an official point of view, no such document should exist – on the other hand, if an Air Marshal chose to reveal clearly what he thought of the ban . . . With such eminence on his side, even though unofficially . . .

Well, why delay? He'd got the job. . . .

He folded the paper carefully, and restored it to his pocket. Then he strode purposefully to the telephone-box. . . .

The Space-Station

Ticker, standing in the mess-room of the hulk, and gazing out of the window, took his breakfast gloomily.

The hulk, as it had become known, even on official memos, was the one habitable spot in thousands of miles of nothing. It was the local office of works, and also the hostel for the men serving their tour of duty. Down its shadow-side, windows ran almost the full length, giving a view of the assembly area. The few ports to sunward were kept shuttered. On the outer sunside of the hull was mounted a ring of parabolic reflectors, none more than a foot across, and all precisely angled. When the eye of the sun shone full in the centre of the ring they were inactive, but it never did for long, and a variation of a degree or two would bring one or other of the reflectors into focus, collecting intense heat. Presently a small, invisible explosion of steam would correct the error by its recoil, and slowly the hulk would swing a little until another reflector came into focus, and gave another correction It went on all the time save for the brief 'nights' in the Earth's shadow, so that the view from the leeward windows never altered: it was always the space-station assembly.

Ticker broke a roll, still warm from the oven operated by a large reflector on the sunside. He left the larger part of it hanging in the air while he buttered the lesser. He munched absent-mindedly, and took a jet of hot coffee. Then he relinquished the plastic coffee-bottle, and let it float while he reached back the rest of the roll before it could waft further. All these actions he performed without conscious thought. They had quickly ceased to be novelties and become part of the natural background conditions to one's tour of duty – so customary that it was, rather, a propensity to poise things conveniently in mid-air when one was at home on leave that had to be checked.

Munching his roll, Ticker continued to regard the view

The Outward Urge

with distaste. However enthusiastic one might be about the project as a whole, a sense of ennui and impatience to be away inevitably set in during the last few days of a spell. It had been so on the verge of his five previous leaves, and this time, for special reasons, it was more pronounced.

Outside, the curve of the Earth made a backdrop to half the window's span, though there was no telling which continent faced him at the moment. Cloud hid the surface and diffused the light as it did most of the time, so that he seemed to be looking, not at a world, but at a segment of a huge pearl resting in a bed of utter blackness. As a foreground, there was the familiar jumble of work in progress.

The main framework of the station had already been welded together, a wheel-like cage of lattice girders, one hundred and forty feet in diameter and twenty-four feet thick. It sparkled in the unobstructed sunlight with a harsh silver glitter that was trying to the eyes. A few panels of the plating were already fixed, and small, bulbous-looking figures in space-suits were manoeuvring more sheets of metal into positions within the framework. The littered, chaotic impression of the whole scene was enhanced by the web of lines which criss-crossed it. Safety-lines and mooring-lines ran in every direction. There were a dozen or more from the hulk to the main assembly, and no single component, section, or instrument was without a tether to fasten it to some other. None of the lines was taut; if one became so, it remained like that for no more than a second or two. Most of them were continually moving in loops, like lazy snakes; others just hung, with barely perceptible motion. Every now and then one of the workers on the framework would pause as a case or an item of the structure as yet unused came nuzzling gently at the girders. He would give it a slight shove, and it would drift away again, its cable coiling in slow-motion behind it.

The Space-Station

A large cylinder, part of the atmosphere regenerating plant, swam into Ticker's view, on its way from the hulk to the assembly. The space-suited man who was ferrying it over had hooked himself to it, and was directing their mutual slow-progress by occasional, carefully aimed blasts from a wide-mouthed pistol. He and his charge were floating free in space but for his thin life-line undulating back to the hulk. There was no sense whatever that all this was taking place as they hurtled round the Earth at a speed of thousands of miles per hour. One was no more aware of it than one was of the pace at which the Earth hurtles round the sun.

Ticker paused in his eating to appreciate the skill of the pistol user; it looked easy, but everyone who had ever tried it knew that it was a great deal easier to set oneself and the load spinning giddily all ways over. That did not happen so often now that the really ham-handed had been weeded out, but a little misjudgement could start it in a moment. He grunted approval, and went on eating, and reflecting....

Four days now, four more days, and he would be back home again.... And how many spells before it would be finished? he wondered. They were holding a sweep on that, with quite a nice prize. The schedules drawn up in comfortable offices back on Earth had gone to pieces at once. In real experience of the conditions progress with the earlier stages had been a great deal slower than the estimates had reckoned. Tricks, techniques, and devices had to be evolved to meet difficulties that the most careful consideration had overlooked. There had also been two bad hold-ups: one, because someone in logistics had made a crass error in the order of dispatch, the other on account of a parcel of girders that had never arrived, and was now presumably circling the Earth as a lonely satellite on its own account – if it had not shot away into space.

The Outward Urge

Working in weightless conditions had also been more troublesome than they had expected. It was true that objects of great bulk and solidity could be shifted by a touch, so that mechanical handling was unnecessary; but on the other hand, there was always the 'equal and opposite reaction' to be considered and dealt with. One was for ever seeking anchorage and purchase before any force whatever could be applied. The lifetime habit of depending on one's weight was only slightly less than an instinct; the mind went on assuming that weight, just as it went on trying to think in terms of 'up and down' until it had been called to order innumerable times.

Ticker left off watching the guided drift of the cylinder, and took a final jet of coffee. He looked at the clock. Still half an hour to go before the shift changed; twenty minutes before he need start getting into his space-suit and testing it. He lit a cigarette, and because there was nothing else to do, found himself moodily contemplating the scene outside once more. The cigarette was half finished when the ship's speaker system grated, and announced:

'Mr Troon please call at the radio-cabin. Radio message for Mr Troon, please.'

Ticker stared at the nearest speaker for an apprehensive moment, and then ground out the remains of his cigarette against the metal wall. With a clicking and scraping of magnetic soles he made his way out of the mess-room. In the passage he disregarded the rules, and sent himself scudding along with a shove. He caught the radio-cabin's door-handle and grounded his feet in one complicated movement. The radio operator looked up.

'Quick worker, Ticker. Here you are.' He handed over a folded piece of paper.

Ticker took it in a hand that irritated him by shaking slightly. The message was brief. It said simply:

The Space-Station

'Happy birthday from Laura and Michael.'

He stood staring at it for some seconds, and then wiped his hand across his forehead. The radio man looked at him thoughtfully.

'Funny things happen in space,' he remarked. 'Must be quite six months since you last had a birthday. Many happy returns, all the same.'

'Er – ah – yes – thanks,' said Ticker vaguely, and pulled himself out of the cabin.

Outside, he stood reading the short message again.

Michael, they had decided, if it were a boy: Anna, for a girl. But early, by at least a fortnight. Still, what did that matter? – except that he had hoped to be on hand. The important thing was 'happy birthday', which meant 'both doing well'.

He became untranced suddenly, and pushed back into the radio-cabin. The dressing-bell for the next shift went while he was scribbling his reply. A few moments later he was whizzing down the passage, headed for the suit-store.

When Ticker's turn came, he stepped to the edge of the open airlock, clipped the eye of his short lead round the guide-line, and then with a two-legged push-off against the side of the hulk, sent himself shooting out along the line towards the assembly. Practice had given all of them a pride in their ability to deal dexterously with the conditions; a quick twist, something like that of a falling cat, brought his feet round to act as buffers at the end of his journey. He unhooked from the guide line, and hooked on to a local life-line, obeying the outside worker's Rule Number One – that he should never for a moment work unattached. Then he pushed across to the far side of the frame where assembly was going on. One of the workers there

The Outward Urge

saw him coming, and turned his head towards him so that his tight-beam radio sounded in Ticker's helmet louder than the all-round reception.

'All yours,' he said. 'And welcome to it. This plate's a bastard.'

Ticker came up to him. They exchanged lines.

'Be seeing you,' said the other, and gave a yank on the line which took him back the way Ticker had come. Ticker shook his new safety-line to send it looping out of his way, and turned to give his consideration to the plate that was a bastard.

The new shift adjusted their general intercom radios to low power so that they could converse comfortably between themselves. They noticed the progress made since their last spell, compared it with the plan, identified the sections at hand, and started in.

Ticker looked his plate over, and then twisted it so that the markings lined up. It was no bastard after all, and slipped quite easily into place. He was not surprised. One got tired, and not infrequently a little stupid, by the end of a shift.

With the plate fixed, he paused, looking out at Earth with his eyeshield raised so that he saw it fully, in all its brilliance – a great shimmering globe that filled half the sky. Quite extensive patches here and there were free of cloud now, and through them there was blue; the sea, perhaps – and then again, perhaps not, for whenever one saw the surface it looked blue, just as the blackness of space seen from the Earth in daylight looked blue.

Somewhere over there, on that great shining ball, he now had a son. The idea came to him as a marvel. He could picture Laura smiling as she held the baby to her. He smiled to himself, and then chuckled. He had smuggled himself a family in spite of the regulations, and if they did find out

The Space-Station

now – he shrugged. And anyway, he had a well-grounded suspicion that he was not the only family man among his supposedly celibate companions. He did not underestimate the Security boys; he simply thought it likely that others besides the Air Marshal found a blind eye convenient. In just four days more – A nudge at his back interrupted him. He turned to find another plate that someone had pushed along for his attention. Gripping a girder between his knees for anchorage, he started to twist it into position.

Half an hour later a tight-beam radio voice from the hulk overrode their local conversation.

'Unidentified object coming up,' it announced, and gave a constellation bearing. The working party's heads turned towards Aries. The great stars flaring there against the multitudinous speckling of the rest looked no different from usual.

'Not a dispatch, you mean?' someone asked.

'Can't be. We've had none notified.'

'Meteor?' someone else suggested, with a trace of uneasiness.

'We don't think so. There's been a slight change of course since radar picked it up a couple of hours ago. That seems to rule out meteors.'

'Can't you get the telescope on it?'

'Only for a glimpse. Damned hulk's hunting too much, we're trying to steady her up.'

'Could it be that parcel of girders, do you think? The lot that went astray. Couldn't it be that its homing gear has just got the range of us?'

'Might be, I suppose,' admitted the voice from the hulk. 'It's certainly got a line straight on us now. If it *is*, the proximity gear should stop it and hold it about a couple of miles off, and you'll need to send somebody out with a line to make it fast. Plenty of time to see about that later. We'll

The Outward Urge

keep you informed, once we can get this damned tub steady enough to keep the glass on it.'

His wave cut off, and the assembly party, after vainly scanning the Aries region again, turned back to their work. Nearly an hour passed before the voice from the hulk spoke once more.

'Hullo there, Assembly!' it said, and without waiting for acknowledgement, went on: 'There's something damned funny about that thing in Aries. It certainly isn't the girder package. We don't know what it is.'

'Well, what's it *look* like?' inquired one of the working party, patiently.

'It's – er – well, it's like a large circle, with three smaller circles set at thirds round the perimeter.'

'You don't say!'

'Well, that's what we see, damn it! The thing's head on to us. The circles may be mile-long cylinders, for all we can tell.'

Again the helmeted heads of the working party turned towards Aries.

'Can't see anything. Is it blasting?'

'There's no sign of blast. It looks as if it's free-falling at us. Just a minute – ' He broke off. Five minutes passed before he came in again. This time his tone was more serious.

'We radioed a description to base, asking for info. and indentification. Their reply is just in. It reads: "No repeat no dispatch you since Number 377K four days ago stop design of object as described not repeat not known here stop Pentagon states not repeat not known them stop consider possible craft/missile hostile stop treat as hostile taking all precautions ends."'

For some moments no one spoke. The helmets of the working party turned as they looked at one another in astonishment.

The Space-Station

'Hostile! For God's sake! Why, every bloody thing out there's hostile,' somebody said.

'Precautions!' said another voice. 'What precautions?'

Ticker inquired:

'Have we any interception missiles?'

'No,' said the voice from the hulk. 'They're scheduled, but they are away down the fitting-out list yet.'

'Hostile?' murmured another voice. 'But who?'

'Who do you think? Who'd rather we didn't have a station out here?'

'But "hostile",' the man said again. 'It would be an act of war – to attack us, I mean.'

'Act of nothing,' said the second man. 'Who even knows we're up here, except the Department; and now, apparently, the Other Fellows. Say we were attacked, and blown up – what'd happen? Sweet damn all. Nothing but hush from both sides. Not even details . . . just hush.'

'Everybody seems to be taking a lot for granted, considering that nobody even knows what the thing is,' someone pointed out.

That, Ticker admitted, was true enough, but somewhat legalistic, for it was difficult to believe that anything could happen to be travelling this particular section of space by sheer accident, and if it were not accidental, then it followed that the intention of any visiting object that did not originate with their Department must be either observatory or hostile.

He turned his head again, surveying the myriad suns that flared in the blackness. The first comment had been right; it was *all* hostile. For a moment he felt that hostility all about him more keenly than at any time since he had first forced himself to push out of the hulk's airlock into nothingness. His memory of that sensation had been dulled, but now, abruptly, he was the intruder again; the presumptuous

The Outward Urge

creature thrusting out of his natural element; precariously self-launched among a wrack of perils. Odd, he thought, in a kind of parenthesis, that it should need the suspicion of human hostility to reawaken the sense of the greater hostility constantly about them.

He became conscious that the others were still talking. Someone had inquired about the object's speed. The hulk was replying:

'Difficult to estimate more than roughly, head on, but doesn't seem to be high, relative to our own. Certainly unlikely to be more than two hundred miles an hour difference, we judge – could well be less. You ought to be able to see it soon. It's starting to catch the earthlight.'

There was no sign of it in the Aries sector yet. Somebody said:

'Should we get back aboard, Skip?'

'No point in it ... It wouldn't help at all if that thing *does* have a homer set on the hulk.'

'True,' agreed someone, and sang gently: ' "Dere's no hidin' place out here." '

They went on working, casting occasional glances into the blackness. Ten minutes later, two men exclaimed simultaneously; they had caught one small, brief flare among the stardust.

'Starboard jet correcting course,' said the voice from the hulk. 'That settles one thing. It's live, and it *is* homing on us. Swinging now. It'll recorrect in a moment.'

They watched intently. Presently, nearly all of them caught a glimpse of the little jet of flame that steadied the object's swing. A man swore:

'God damn it! And us here, like sitting pigeons. One little guided missile to meet it. That's all that's needed. Pity one of the Department's great brains didn't allow for that, isn't it?'

The Space-Station

'What about an oxygen tube?' someone suggested. 'Fix up one of the dispatch homers on it, and let it jet itself along till they meet.'

'Good idea – if we had a day or so to fix the homer,' agreed another.

Presently the object caught more of the earthlight, and they were able to keep its location marked, though not yet able to distinguish its shape. A consultation went on between the leader of the working party and the commander of the hulk. It was decided not to take the party inboard. If the thing were indeed a missile and set to explode on contact or at close proximity, then the situation would be equally hopeless wherever one was; but should it, on the other hand, fail to explode on contact and simply cause impact damage to the hulk, it might be useful to have the party outside, ready to give what help it could.

On that decision, the men in space-suits started to push themselves off, and drift through the web of girders towards the hulkward side of the assembly. There they exchanged their local safety-lines for others attached to the hulk, and were ready to pull themselves across, if necessary.

They waited in an uneasy group, a surrealist cluster of grotesque figures anchored to the framework at eccentric angles by their magnetic soles while they watched the oncoming object, the 'craft/missile' grow slowly larger.

Soon they could distinguish the outline described; three small circles set about a larger. It was from the small circles that a correcting puff of flame came now and then.

'It's my guess, from the general look of the thing and its slow speed,' the hulk Commander's voice said, dispassionately, 'that it's half-missile, half-mine; a kind of hunting mine. I'd guess, too, by the way it is aligned on us that it is a contact type. Might be chemical, or nuclear – probably chemical; if it were nuclear a proximity fuse would be

The Outward Urge

good enough. Besides, a nuclear explosion would be detectable from Earth. With a chemical explosion out here you'd want all the concentration of force you can get – hence contact.'

No one seemed disposed to question the Commander's deductions. There could be no doubt that it was aligned on them. The swinging was so slight that they could see no more than the head-on view.

'Estimated relative speed about one hundred and twenty miles an hour,' added the Commander.

Slow, Ticker thought, very slow – probably to keep manoeuvrability in case of evasive action by its target. There was nothing one could do but stand there and wait for it.

'E.T.A. now five minutes,' the voice from the hulk told them, calmly.

They waited.

Ticker found a new understanding of the stringent security regulations. Hitherto, he had taken it for granted that their purpose was to preserve the lead. Clearly, once it should be known that any nation had a space-station under construction, those who had it only in the drawing-board stage would press on, and the pace would grow warmer. The best way to avoid that was secrecy, and if necessary to show astonishment that any such device was being seriously contemplated. That had seemed reasonable; there was nothing to be gained by creating a situation where construction would have to be rushed, and possibly a lot might be lost by it. The thought of an attack on the station before it was even finished had never occurred to him.

But if this were indeed a missile, and if it should get the hulk, nobody would survive. And if the Department were to be stung into denouncing the aggression? Well, the Other Fellows would just shrug and deny. 'What, us! Why, we

The Space-Station

never even knew it existed. Obviously an accident,' they would say. 'An accident which has now been followed by a vicious and despicable slander in an effort to cover up those responsible.'

'Three minutes,' said the Commander.

Ticker took his eyes from the 'craft/missile' and looked about him. His gaze loitered on the moon, a clear, sharp coin, recently risen from behind the blue pearl of Earth. Scarred but serene, it hung on the sky; a silver medal, still waiting to be won. The next leap.

First there had been this little hop of ten thousand miles to make a stepping-stone for the leap of two hundred and twenty-four thousand miles, more or less – and then, not in his time, but some day, there would be still greater leaps beyond. For him, for now, the moon would be enough.

'The moon,' murmured Ticker. ' "The moon on the one hand, the dawn on the other: the moon is my sister, the dawn is my brother." '

Suddenly he was swept with a shaking anger. A fury against stupidity and littleness, against narrow, scheming minds that were ready to wreck the greatest adventure of all, as a political move. What would happen now if their work were destroyed? The cost had been in proportion to the ambition. If all this were lost, would the government be willing, could they even afford, to make a new allocation and start again? Might it not be that, with such an example, all the rival nations would content themselves with arrangements to blow any other attempted space-stations out of existence? Would that be the end of the great adventure – to be kept earthbound by stalemate and futility ...?

'Two minutes,' said the voice.

Ticker looked at the missile again. It was swinging a little more now, enough to give glimpses of length, instead of a flat diagram of circles. He watched it curiously. There was

The Outward Urge

no doubt that the roving action was increasing. Correction and re-correction were stronger and more frequent.

'What's happening to the bastard?' a voice asked. 'Kind of losing its touch, isn't it?'

They stared at it in horrid fascination, watching the yawing motion grow wider while the correcting jets spat more fiercely and rapidly. Soon it was swinging so much that they were getting broadside views of it – a fat, droplet-shaped body, buttressed by three smaller droplet shapes which housed its driving tubes. The small correcting tubes, so busily employed at this moment, branched laterally in radial clumps from the main-tube nacelles. Its method of working was obvious. Once the homing device had found a line on the target the main tubes would fire to give directional impetus. Then, either to keep down to manoeuvrable speed, or simply to economize, they would cut out, leaving it to coast easily to the target while the homer kept it on course by correcting touches from the side tubes. Less obvious was what had got into it now, and was causing it to bear down on them in a wildly drunken wobble.

'Why the devil should it go nuts and start "hunting" at this stage?' muttered the leader of the working party.

'That's *it*,' said the Commander from the hulk, with a sudden hopeful note in his voice. 'It *has* gone nuts; all bewitched and bewildered. It's the masses, don't you see? The mass of the hulk is about the same as that of the assembly and parts now. The thing is approaching on a line where they are both equidistant. Its computers are foozled: they can't decide which to go for. It would be bloody funny if it weren't serious. If it can't decide in another few seconds at that speed it'll overshoot any possibility of correcting in time.'

They kept watching the thing tensely. It had, in fact,

The Space-Station

already lost a little speed, for it was now yawing so widely that the steering tubes' attempts to correct the swing were having some braking effect. For a half minute there was silence. Then someone breathed out, noisily.

'He's right, by God! It *is* going to miss,' he said.

Other held breaths were released, and the earphones sounded a huge, composite sigh of relief. It was no longer possible to doubt that the missile would pass right between the hulk and the assembly.

In a final desperate effort to steady up, the port tubes fired a salvo that spun it right round on its own axis as it hurtled along.

'Bloody thing's started waltzing now,' observed a voice.

Still wobbling wildly it careered on, in a flaring, soundless rush. Closer it reeled, and closer, until it was whirling madly past, between them and the hulk.

Ticker did not see what happened next. There was a sudden violent shock which banged his head against the inside of his helmet, and turned everything into dancing lights. For a few seconds he was dazed. Then it came to him that he was no longer holding on to the framework of the assembly. He groped, and found nothing. With an effort, he opened his eyes and forced them into focus. The first thing they showed him was the hulk and the half-built space-station dwindling rapidly in the distance.

Ticker kicked wildly, and managed to turn himself round, but it took him several moments to grasp what had happened. He found that he was floating in space in company with a collection of minor parts of the assembly and two other space-suited men, while, close by, the missile, now encumbered with a tangle of lines, was still firing its steering tubes while it cavorted and spun in an imbecilic fashion. By degrees he perceived that the missile had in its passage managed to entangle itself in a dozen or more tethers and safety-lines, and torn them away, together with whatever happened to be attached to them.

He closed his eyes for a moment. His head throbbed. He fancied that it was bleeding on the right side. He hoped the cut was small; if there was much blood it might float around loose in his helmet and get into his eyes. Suddenly the Commander's voice in the phone said:

'Quiet everyone.' It paused, and went on: 'Hullo, hullo there! Calling you three with the missile. Are you all right? Are you all right?'

Ticker ran his tongue over his lips, and swallowed.

'Hullo, Skipper. Ticker here. I'm all right, Skip.'

'You don't sound so all right, Ticker.'

'Bit muzzy. Knocked my head on my helmet. Better in a minute.'

'What about the other two?'

A groggy voice broke in:

'Nobby here, Skipper. I'm all right, too – I think. Been sick as a dog – not funny at all. Don't know about the other. Who is it?'

'Must be Dobbin. Hullo there, Dobbin! Are you all right?'

There was no reply.

'It was a hell of a jerk, Skipper,' said the groggy voice.

'How's your air?'

Ticker looked at the dials.

'Normal supply, and reserve intact,' he said.

'My reserve isn't registering. Fractured, maybe, but I've got nearly four hours,' said Nobby.

'Better cut loose, and make your way back by hand tubes,' said the Commander. 'You right away, Nobby. Ticker, you've got more air. Can you reach Dobbin? If you can, link him on to you, and bring him back with you. Think you can?'

The Space-Station

'Shouldn't be difficult, I think.'

'Look, Skip – ' Nobby began.

'That's an order, Nobby,' the Commander told him briefly.

Kicking himself over, Ticker was able to see one of the space-suited figures fumbling at its belt. Presently the safety-line floated free, though the figure still kept along in company. It drew the pistol-like hand-tube from the holster, and held it in front with both hands, kicking a little as it manoeuvred to get the hulk dead behind it in the tube's mirror-sights. Then the tube flared, and the figure holding it dropped away, slowly at first, then with increasing speed.

'Be seeing you, Ticker,' said its voice. 'Bacon and eggs?'

'Done both sides, mind,' Ticker told him.

He drew his own tube. When he had the second space-suited figure in the mirror, he gave the briefest possible touch on the trigger to set himself drifting towards it. A few moments later he reported:

'I'm afraid old Dobbin's through, Skip. It was quick, though. Bloody great rip in the left leg of his suit. Damn bad luck. Shall I bring him back?'

The Commander hesitated a moment.

'No, Ticker,' he decided. 'It'd just mean an additional hazard for you. Dobbin wouldn't want that. No, cast off his line and let him go, poor chap. Take his reserve air bottle, though – and his tube, too. It'll help you to catch up on Nobby.'

There was a brief silence, then:

'That's funny,' Ticker murmured.

'What's funny?' demanded the Commander.

'Just a minute, Skip.'

'What *is* it, Ticker?'

'The lines have tightened, Skipper. A minute ago, we and the odd bits were all in a clump, with the missile acting

The Outward Urge

daft alongside. Now it's steadied up, seems to be pulling away. Hell, this is confusing – you aren't where you ought to be, either. The – oh, I get it. The thing's turning; swinging us round after it. . . . I'm letting old Dobbin go now . . .' There was a pause. 'He's drifting off on a different line, away from me. The thing must be making a wide turn, I think. Difficult to tell just what it is doing; it's giving lots of little bursts as it steadies up. I don't care much for this, Skipper. All the towed bits, including me, have swung together in a jumble.'

'Better cast off now, and shove yourself clear.'

'Just a minute, Skip. I want to see – ' His voice tailed away. 'Yes, yes, she is. She's pulling, pulling steadily round. . . .'

Ticker was hanging out at the end of his life-line, watching the constellations wheel slowly, and twisting slowly himself, which made it the more confusing.

The random element introduced into the missile by the conflict of purpose had been sorted out. It was coordinated again, and its change of direction was steady, smooth, and purposeful. It was, in fact, back on the job. Its radar had searched for, and found, the target it had missed in its temporary derangement, and was bringing it round to bear once more. Somewhere inside the fat metal droplet there were relays ready to go in once it was steady in the aim; a brief burst on the main tubes would send it back to the attack. . . .

'My God!' exclaimed Ticker, and began to haul himself hand over hand along his safety-line, shoving aside the trailing flotsam of assembly items as he went; and making for the missile itself.

'What's that about? Haven't you cast off yet?' inquired the Commander.

Ticker did not reply. He had come close to the missile,

The Space-Station

swung a little out from it by the continuing turn, but able to reach it. Presently he could touch it, and brought round a leg to kick himself clear of the steering-tubes. He pulled himself forward on the length of line remaining, and caught hold of the member which joined one of the nacelles to the main body. It was round all three of these members that the lines had tangled as the missile had swept past the assembly, and he tied his safety-line short to a loop in the tangle that looked as if it would hold.

'What the devil are you doing, Ticker?' asked the Commander.

'I'm aboard the missile, Skipper,' Ticker told him.

'For heaven's sake! – you mean you're *on* the damned thing? Look, I told you to cast off. Do I have to make it an order?'

'I hope you won't, Skipper, because I rather think that if you did, and if I obeyed it, I'd very likely have nowhere to go.'

'What do you mean by that?'

'Well, it looks to me as if this thing is in the process of getting round to have another go at you.'

'Is it, by hell! You sure of that, Ticker?'

''Fraid so. Don't see what else it can be doing. It's certainly making a steady arc, and if that's its game, this seems to be as good a place as any.'

'Wouldn't be my choice. What do you mean?'

'Well, if I'd stayed where I was I'd be fried when it fires its main tubes. And if I cast off now and it does go for you, I stand to die slowly in a space-suit. Not nice, at all. Whereas this way I get a free ride home. If it misses you, I can roll off: if it doesn't, well, it'll be the same for all of us. . . .'

'That's a lot more logical than agreeable. What's it doing now?'

'Still coming round. You lie to port as we go. About

The Outward Urge

twenty degrees more to swing yet. You should be able to observe easily.'

'We've got you on the radar, all right, but we can't bring the glass to bear so far to sunward.'

'I see. Try to keep you informed,' said Ticker.

He worked forward on the metal body. There was enough iron in it to give some traction for his magnetic soles. 'Turn still gradual, but steady,' he reported. 'This thing has a number of knobs and protuberances and so on round the nose,' he added. 'Five major and several minor. God knows what they are. One or more must be radar.'

'With limited range, obviously,' said the Commander. 'Must be, or it would go off chasing the moon, or the Earth, instead of us. That looks as if they must know our distance and the plane of our orbit pretty accurately, damn them. Given that, it wouldn't be too difficult to make it sure to find us sooner or later. If you can sort out which is the radar, it might be helpful to have a good bash at it.'

'Trouble is they aren't like anything I've ever seen,' complained Ticker. 'It'd be just too bad if the one I bashed turned out to be a fuse.'

'Take your time, and make sure. How's she bearing now?'

'Nearly on. Three or four degrees more.'

He slid back a bit to a position where he could brace himself on a nacelle member. The intermittent vibration from the starboard tubes ceased, and a new tremor ran through the missile as the port tubes fired to check her.

'She's round now,' he told the Commander. 'Lined up on you, and steadying.'

He waited tensely, gripping with arms and knees as best he could. The main tubes spurted briefly. He felt the missile surge forward. There was a jerk as the lines to the flotsam tightened, and checked it. The tubes fired again. The missile

The Space-Station

and its tow jerked to and fro on their loose coupling, but only one of the lines parted, to let a girder section spin off into space on its own. The rest joggled, and the lines looped about until presently the whole conglomeration was in motion on the new line, headed now for the distant hulk, but at a speed somewhat below that of the missile's former attack.

'On our way now, Skip,' Ticker reported. 'I'll get forward again, and try to see about that radar.'

On the nose once more, he tried shielding the protuberances in turn with his gloved hands. There was no apparent effect; certainly no tendency to deviate from the course. He slackened off the life-line a little, and hung over the front to shield as many as possible at once with his body, also without noticeable result. Again he examined the projections. One of them looked as if it might be a small solar-energy cell, but the rest were unidentifiable. He was sure only that some of them must be relaying information to the controls. He sat back, astride the nose of the missile, and feeling the need of a cigarette as he had seldom felt it before.

'Got me beat,' he admitted. 'I just don't know, Skip. Almost any of them might be any damned thing.'

He turned his attention to the spangled blackness about him. The hulk and the assembly, lying dead ahead, were shining more brightly than anything but the sun itself.

'One thing, Skipper,' he said. 'It won't be like the other try. The turn's brought it round so that you and the assembly are almost in line from here.'

'There must be some way of disabling or disarming the brute. Don't any of those projections unscrew?'

'A couple of them look as if they ought to, but I've no spanners, and I lost the grips when I was snatched off.'

The Outward Urge

Moving forward again, he braced himself as well as he could, and tried to unscrew a graspable portion with his gloved hands. It was a waste of effort. He gave up, and gazed ahead while he recovered his breath. The missile was steady on its course, with barely a tremor of correction to be felt. Distance was difficult to judge, but he guessed that he could not be much more than twenty miles from the hulk. Not many minutes . . .

Ticker became aware of sweat forming on his forehead, and stinging in the corners of his eyes. He shook his head, and worked his eyebrows to try to get rid of the drops. Presently he slithered clumsily back to the member connecting the port nacelle. He sat on it, lashing himself there as best he could with the life-line. He pressed back on the main body, bracing his feet against the nacelle itself. He drew the two hand-tubes, his own and Dobbin's. He checked their power settings, and then held them on either side of him, their wide mouths pointing outwards, their butts firmly grounded against the metal casing at his back. Like that, he waited.

'Ticker. Bale out now,' said the Commander.

'I told you, Skip. I'm not for dying slowly in a space-suit.'

The hulk, and the assembly beyond it, seemed to be rushing towards him now. His spine was prickling, partly with sweat, partly with the knowledge of the explosive just behind it. He found himself becoming more conscious of it, crawlingly aware of the vast tearing power held in a thin shell, waiting for the impact that would release it. The sweat ran out of every pore, soaking his clothes.

He sat with his head turned to the right, watching the hulk grow bigger and nearer from eyes that stung with salt. 'Not too soon,' he told himself. 'It mustn't be too soon.' But it mustn't be too late, either. He was aware of the Commander's voice in the phone again, but he took no notice

The Space-Station

of it. Would one mile distance do? – Or would that not be soon enough? No, it should give him just time enough at the rate he was going. He would make it one mile as near as he could judge. ... He went on watching, both hands clenched on the tube-grips ...

Must be about a couple of miles now....

He set his teeth, and pulled both triggers right back for a moment. ... The hulk seemed to slide to the left as the missile kicked over more sharply than he had expected. The thing keeled for a moment, like a dancer caught off balance. Then the steering-tubes fired a correcting blast. The nose swung back on to the target, and then beyond it. The tubes on the near-side fired to correct the overswing: at the same moment Ticker pulled both triggers back, and held them there. With the combined blast reinforcing her new backswing, the missile leapt sideways and swung broadside to her course at the same time. The constellations whirled round Ticker's head. He looked wildly round for the hulk, and found it back over his left shoulder – and not much more than half a mile away. He prayed that there was not time enough for a correction....

An air missile, with air to grip, and fins to grip it, might have managed a quick correction; but in space, where every movement is a delicate matter of thrust and counter-thrust, time too is a highly important factor: oscillation cannot be killed at a stroke, lost equilibrium cannot be regained in a moment ...

The angle of diversion needed to get back on course grew more acute every second. Ticker knew suddenly that the thing could not do it. Only the main drive could have exerted enough force to jump it back in time to hit – and experience showed that the main drive liked to be steady in the aim before it fired.

But the side-tubes tried. Ticker braced himself where he

The Outward Urge

sat while the heavens reeled as the missile spun. Then the hulk rushed past in a blur, fifty yards away . . .

'Done it, by God! Bloody good show, Ticker!' said a voice.

'Quiet there!' snapped the Commander. 'Ticker, that was magnificent. Now come off it. Bale out quick.'

Ticker, still held by his line, relaxed, feeling all in. The missile, still swinging from side to side, scudded on with him into space.

'Ticker, do you hear me? Bale out!' repeated the Commander.

Ticker said wearily:

'I hear you, Skip. But there won't be enough power left in these tubes to get me back to you.'

'Never mind. Use what there is as a brake. We'll fetch you in. But get clear of it *now*!'

There was a pause. Ticker's tired voice said:

'Sorry, Skip. But we don't know what this bastard's going to do next, do we?'

'For heaven's sake, man . . .'

'Sorry, Skip. Mutiny, I'm afraid.'

Ticker rested as he was, with his eyes closed. The sight of the constellations swooping to the missile's swings was making him feel sick. He was tired out, his head ached badly, he was soaked through with sweat, it was an effort to think. He sat as he was until he became aware that the pull on the line that held him in place had changed, and become constant. He opened his eyes, and found himself looking full at the moon.

It was sliding slowly leftwards, and the great curve of the Earth was rising on his right.

'She's going about again,' he said drearily. 'I wonder if these bastards ever run out of fuel?'

Looking down, he found that he was still gripping the

The Space-Station

hand-tubes. He let them go, and float on their safety-cords while his gloved hands fumbled at the knot of the line which held him. He managed to slacken it off, and dragged himself back on to the main body again. The thing was fairly steady once more, with the starboard tubes firing now and then to turn it; there could be little doubt that it was in the process of coming round for yet another attack. He pulled himself forward on to the nose again, and sat astride of it, holding on to the projecting knobs.

Perched there, and summoning up his strength, he looked about him. Under his left foot lay the pearl-like Earth, with the night-shadow beginning to creep across her. The sun blazed high to his right. Up to the left the pallid moon lay in a bed of jet scattered with diamond dust.

Lower to his left, but sliding slowly round towards the front, floated the hulk and the glittering spider-work of girders that would one day be the space-station.

Once more he turned his eyes down to the great globe creeping past his left foot. He watched it steadily for some moments; then he lifted his right hand, and turned the air supply up a little.

'Skipper?' he inquired.

'Receiving you, Ticker,' acknowledged the Commander. 'We've just managed to get the glass on you. What the hell do you think you're doing?'

'I'm going to have a shot at disabling the thing, Skip. I think the line is to have a bash at this short, thick rod-thing in front of me. Can you see it?'

'Yes. I can see it. Might be anything. You're satisfied it's part of the radar gear?'

'Obvious, Skipper.'

'Ticker, you're lying. Leave it alone.'

'Might be able to dent it a bit. Enough to mess it up.'

'Ticker – '

The Outward Urge

'I know what I'm doing, Skip. Here goes.'

Ticker hooked his toes under two of the projections, and gripped with his knees, for the best possible purchase. He took up the hand-tubes, one in each hand, and slammed away at the short, thick rod with all his might. Presently he paused, panting.

'No damned weight. Like hitting with matchsticks,' he complained. 'Not a mark on it.'

He turned the air on a little more, and screwed up his eyes to squeeze the sweat out of them. The missile was still coming round in its big curve. Twenty degrees more would bring it on to the line of attack again.

'Going to try another of them this time,' he said, lifting the tubes once more.

Through the telescope the Commander watched him start to belabour one of the more slender projections: from the right, from the left, from the right, from the ...

There was a flash so brilliant that it stung his eyes.

That was all: a vivid, silent flash shining for its brief moment as brightly as the sun. ...

Then, where it had been, the glass showed nothing but empty darkness, with small, uncaring stars, thousands of light-years beyond. ...

The Air Marshal spread the message on his desk, and studied it for several long, thoughtful moments.

His mind went back to the night fifty years ago when the other Ticker had not come back. The same job for grandson as for grandfather. Only it had been easier the first time, with a war on, and the news half-expected. He felt old. He *was* old. Too old, perhaps. If they had not changed the regulations he would have been on the shelf ten years ago at his age. ...

Still, here he was. And he'd tell her himself. Tell this poor

The Space-Station

girl – just as he had told the other one, long ago. So piteously little he could tell her. ... Lost on a secret mission ... So cruelly blank ...

She would know later on, of course – when Security considered it safe. Oh, yes, she would know. He'd see to that. He would throw all his weight there. ... For sheer cold courage ... Nothing less than a V.C. ... Nothing less ...

He looked back at the security report for the previous day.

'Subject dispatched radio to Troon. Message: "Happy birthday from Laura and Michael." (*N.B.* Presumed code reference to subject's birth of child, male, on previous evening. Supporting this: (*a*) Troon's birthday 8 May; (*b*) his radio reply: "I love you both.")'

The Air Marshal sighed, and shook his head.

'But at least she has the boy,' he murmured. 'And she knows he knew about the boy. ... I'm glad he did. ... The old Ticker never even knew there was to be a child ...

'I hope they meet up there. ... Ought to get on well together. ...'

TWO

THE MOON

A.D. 2044

THERE was a double knock on the alloy door. The Station-Commander, standing with his back to the room, looking out of the window, appeared for the moment not to hear it. Then he turned, just as the knock was repeated.

'Come in,' he said, in a flat unwelcoming tone.

The woman who entered was tall, well-built, and aged about thirty. Her good looks were a trifle austere, but softened slightly by the curls of her short, light-brown hair. Her most striking feature was her soft, blue-grey eyes; they were beautiful, and intelligent too.

'Good morning, Commander,' she said, in a brisk, formal voice.

He waited until the door had latched, then:

'You'll probably be ostracized,' he told her.

She shook her head slightly. 'My official duty,' she said. 'Doctors are different. Privileged in some ways, on account of being not quite human in others.'

He watched her come further into the room, wondering, as he had before, whether she had originally joined the service because its silky uniform matched her eyes, for she could certainly have advanced more quickly elsewhere. Anyway the uniform certainly suited her elegant slenderness.

'Am I not invited to sit?' she inquired.

'By all means you are, if you care to. I thought you might prefer not,' he told her.

She approached a chair with the half-floating step that

The Moon

had become second nature, and let herself sink gently on to it. Without removing her gaze from his face, she pulled out a cigarette-case.

'Sorry,' he said, and held the box from the desk towards her. She took one, let him light it for her, and blew the smoke out in a leisurely way.

'Well, what is it?' he asked, with a touch of irritation.

Still looking at him steadily, she said:

'You know well enough what it is, Michael. It is that this *will not do*.'

He frowned.

'Ellen, I'll be glad if you'll keep out of it. If there is one person on this station who is not directly involved, it is you.'

'Nonsense, Michael. There is *not* one person. But it is just because I am the least involved that I have come to talk to you. Somebody *has* to talk to you. You can't afford just to let the pressure go on rising while you stay in here, like Achilles sulking in his tent.'

'A poor simile, Ellen. *I* have not quarrelled with my leader. It is the rest who have quarrelled with theirs – with me.'

'That's not the way they see it, Michael.'

He turned, and walked over to the window again. Standing there, with his face pale in the bright earth light, he said:

'I know what they are thinking. They've shown it plainly enough. There's a pane of ice between us. The Station-Commander is now a pariah.

'All the old scores have come up to the surface. I am Ticker Troon's son – the man who got there by easy preferment. For the same reason I'm *still* here, at the age of fifty – five years over the usual grounding age; and keeping younger men from promotion. I'm known to be in bad with half a dozen politicians and much of the top brass in the

The Outward Urge

Space-House. Not to be trusted in my judgement because I'm an enthusiast – i.e. a man with a one-track mind. Would have been thrown out years ago if they had dared to face the outcry – Ticker Troon's son, again. And now there's this.'

'Michael,' she said calmly. 'Just why are you letting this get you down? What's behind it?'

He looked hard at her for a moment before he said, with a touch of suspicion:

'What do you mean?'

'Simply what I say – what is behind this uncharacteristic outburst? You are perfectly well aware that if you had not earned your rank you would not be here – you'd have been harmlessly stowed away at a desk somewhere, years ago. As for the rest – well, it's mostly true. But the self-pity angle isn't like you. You *could* simply have cashed in and lain back comfortably for life on the strength of being Ticker Troon's son, but you didn't. You took the name he left you into your hand, and you deliberately *used* it for a weapon. It was a good weapon, and of course it made enemies for you, so of course they maligned you. But you know, and hundreds of thousands of people know, that if you had not used it as you did we should not be here today: there wouldn't be any British Moon Station: and your father would have sacrificed himself for nothing.'

'Self-pity – ' he began, indignantly.

'Phony self-pity,' she corrected, looking at him steadily.

He turned away.

'Would you like to tell me what the proper feeling is when, at a time of crisis, the men that you have worked with and for – men that you thought had loyalty and respect, even some affection, for you, turn icy cold, and send you to coventry? It certainly is not the time to feel pride of achievement, is it?'

The Moon

She let the question hang for a moment, then:

'Understanding?' she suggested. 'A more sympathetic consideration of the other man's point of view – and the state of his mind, perhaps?' She paused for several seconds. 'We are none of us in a normal state of mind,' she went on. 'There is far too much emotion compressed in this place for anyone's judgement to be quite rational. It's harder for some than for others. *And* we don't all have quite the same things uppermost in our minds,' she added.

Troon made no reply. He continued to stand with his back to her, gazing steadily out of the window. Presently, she walked across to stand beside him.

The view outside was bleak. In the foreground an utterly barren plain; a flatness broken only by various-sized chunks of rock, and occasionally the rim of a small crater. The harshness of it was hard on the eyes; the lit surfaces so bright, the shadows so stygian that, if one looked at any one part too long, it dazzled and seemed to dance about.

Beyond the plain, the mountains stuck up like cardboard cut-outs. Eyes accustomed to the weathered mountains of Earth found the sharpness, the height, the vivid jaggedness of them disturbing. Newcomers were always awed, and usually frightened, by them. 'A dead world,' they always said, as they looked on the view for the first time, and they said it in hushed voices, with a feeling that they were seeing the ultimate dreadful place.

Too facile, too earthbound a sensation, Troon often thought. Death implied corruption, decay, and change, but on the moon there was nothing to corrupt, nothing that could change. There was only the impersonal savagery of nature, random, eternal, frozen, and senseless. Something that the Greeks had glimpsed in their conception of Chaos.

Over the horizon to the right hung a fluorescent quarter-segment of the Earth; a wide wedge bounded on one side by the night line, and serrated at the base by the bare teeth of the mountains.

For more than a minute Troon gazed at its cold, misted blue light before he spoke. Then:

'The idiot's delight,' he said.

The doctor nodded slowly.

'Without doubt,' she agreed. 'And there – there we have it, don't we?'

She turned away from the window and went back to the chair.

'I know,' she said, 'or perhaps I should say, I like to think I know, what this place means to you. You fought to establish it; and then you had to fight to maintain it. It has been your job in life; the purpose of your existence; the second foothold on the outward journey. Your father died for it; you have lived for it. You have mothered, more than fathered, an ideal: and you have to learn, as mothers learn, that there has to be a weaning.

'Now, up there, there is war. It has been going on for ten days – at God knows what cost: the worst war in history – perhaps even the last. Great cities are holes in the ground; whole countries are black ashes; seas have boiled up in vapour, and fallen as lethal rain. But still new pillars of smoke spring up, new lakes of fire spread out, and more millions of people die.

' "The idiot's delight", you say. But to what extent are you saying that because you hate it for what it is; and to what extent are you saying it from fear that your work will be ruined – that there may come some turn of events that will drive us off the moon?'

Troon walked slowly back, and seated himself on a corner of the desk.

'All reasons for hating war are good,' he said, 'but some are better than others. If you hate it and want to abolish

The Moon

it simply because it kills people – well, there are a number of popular inventions, the car and the aeroplane, for instance, that you might do well to abolish for the same reason. It is cruel and evil to kill people – but their deaths in war are a symptom, not a cause. I hate war partly because it is stupid – which it has been for a long time – but still more because it has recently become *too* stupid, and too wasteful, and too dangerous.'

'I agree. And then, too, of course, much of what it wastes could otherwise be used to further Project Space.'

'Certainly, and why not? Here we are at last, close to the threshold of the universe, with the greatest adventure of the human race just ahead of us, and still this witless, parochial bickering goes on – getting nearer to race suicide every time it flares up.'

'And yet,' she pointed out, 'if it were not for the requirements of strategy we should not be here now.'

He shook his head.

'Strategy is the ostensible reason perhaps, but it is not the *only* reason. We are here because the quintessential quality of our age is that of dreams coming true. Just think of it. For centuries we have dreamt of flying; recently we made that come true: we have always hankered for speed; now we have speeds greater than we can stand: we wanted to speak to far parts of the Earth; we can: we wanted to explore the sea bottom; we have: and so on, and so on: and, too, we wanted the power to smash our enemies utterly; we have it. If we had truly wanted peace, we should have had that as well. But true peace has never been one of the genuine dreams – we have got little further than preaching against war in order to appease our consciences. The truly wishful dreams, the many-minded dreams are now irresistible – they become facts.

'We may reach them deviously, and almost always they

The Outward Urge

have an undesired obverse; we learnt to fly, and carried bombs; we speed, and destroy thousands of our fellow men; we broadcast, and we can lie to the whole world. We can smash our enemies, but if we do we shall smash ourselves. And some of the dreams have pretty queer midwives, but they get born all the same.'

Ellen nodded slowly.

'And reaching for the moon was one of what you call the truly wishful dreams?'

'Of course. For the moon, first; and then, one day, for the stars. This is a realization. But there' – he pointed out of the window at the Earth – 'down there they are seeing us as a hateful silver crescent which they fear – that is the obverse of this particular dream.

'Nobody hated the moon until we reached it. For thousands of years it has been worshipped, honoured, and played to. Lovers sighed to it, children cried for it. It was Isis, and Diana, it was Selene, kissing her sleeping Endymion – and now we have identified it with Siva, the destroyer. So they are hating it now, because of us; and well they may. We have violated an ancient mystery, shattered an infinite serenity, trampled down antique myths, and smeared its face with blood.

'*That* is the obverse, ugly and ignoble. Yet it is better that it should have been done at this cost than that it should not have been done at all. Most births are painful, and none are pretty."

'You're very eloquent,' said the doctor, a little wondering.

'Aren't you, on your own subject?'

'But would you be telling me, in an elaborate way, that the end justifies the means?'

'I am not interested in justifying. I am simply saying that certain practices which may be unpleasant in themselves

The Moon

can produce results which are not. There is many a flower which would not be growing if the dung had not happened to fall where it did. The Romans built their empire with savage cruelty, but it did make European civilization possible; because America prospered on slave labour, she was able to achieve independence; and so on. And now, because the armed forces wanted a position of strategic advantage, they have enabled us to start out into space.'

'To you, then, this station' – she waved an encompassing hand – 'this is simply a jumping-off place for the planets?'

'Not simply,' he told her. 'At present it is a strategic outpost – but its potentialities are far more significant.'

'Far more important, you mean?'

'As I see it – yes.'

The doctor lit a cigarette, and considered in silence for a few moments. Then she said:

'There seems to me very little doubt that most people here have a pretty accurate idea of your scale of values, Michael. It would not be news to you, I suppose, that with the exception of three or four – and the Astronomical Section which is starry-eyed, anyway – almost nobody shares them?'

'It would not,' he said. 'It has not been, for years; but it is only lately that it has become a matter of uncomfortable importance. Even so, millions of people *can* be wrong – and often have been.'

She nodded, and went on, equably:

'Well, suppose we take a look at it from their point of view. All the people here volunteered, and were posted here as a garrison. They did not, and they do not, consider it primarily as a jumping-off place – though I suppose some of them think it may become that one day – now, at this moment, they are seeing it as what it was established to be

The Outward Urge

– a Bombardment Station: a strategic position from which a missile can be placed within a five-mile circle drawn anywhere on Earth. That, they say, and quite truly say, is the reason for the station's existence; and the purpose for which it is equipped. It was built – just as the other Moon Stations were built – to be a threat. It was hoped that they would never be used, simply because the knowledge of their existence would be an incentive to keep the peace.

'Well, that hope has been wiped out. God knows who, or what, really started this war, but it has come. And what happened? The Russian Station launched a salvo of missiles. The American Station began pumping out a systematic bombardment. The moon, in fact, went into action. But what part did the British Station play in this action? It sent off just three medium-weight missiles!

'The American Station spotted that Russian freighter-rocket coming in, and got it, with a light missile. The Russian Station – and, by the look of it, one of the Russian Satellites – thereupon hammered the American Station, which erupted missiles for a time, both local and earthward-bound, and then suddenly went quiet. The Russian Station kept on sending missiles at intervals for a time, then it, too, went quiet.

'And what were we doing while all this was going on? We were sending off three more medium-sized missiles. And since the Russian Station stopped, we have contributed another three.

'*Nine medium-sized missiles!* Our total part in the war, to date!

'Meanwhile, the real war goes on up there. And what's happening in it? Nobody knows. One minute's news is corrected, or denied, a few minutes later. There's propaganda to hearten, propaganda to dishearten; there's wishful thinking, obvious lying, clever lying, incoherence, and

The Moon

hysteria. There may even be a few grains of truth somewhere, but nobody knows which they are.

'All we *do* know for sure is that the two greatest powers there have ever been are out to destroy one another with every weapon they possess. Hundreds of cities and towns must have vanished, and all the people in them. Whole continents are being scorched and ruined.

'Is either side winning? *Can* either side win? Will there be anything left? What has happened to our own country, and our homes? We *don't know!*

'And we do nothing! We just sit out here, and look at the Earth, all calm and pearly-blue, and wonder hour after hour – day after day, now – what horrors are going on under the clouds. Thinking about our families and friends, and what may have happened to them....

'The wonder to me is that so few of us, as yet, have cracked up. But I warn you, professionally, that if things go on like this, more of us will before long...

'*Of course* the men brood, and become more desperate and rebellious as it goes on. *Of course* they ask themselves what we are here for at all, if not to be used. Why have we not fired our big missiles? Perhaps they would not count a great deal in the scale of things, but they'd be something: we'd be doing what we can. They were the reason we were sent here – so why haven't we fired them? Why didn't we fire them at the beginning, when they would have had most effect? The other stations did. Why have we still not fired them, even now? Can you tell us that?'

She ended, looking at him steadily. He looked back at her, just as steadily.

'I don't plan strategy,' he said. 'It is not my job to understand top-level decisions. I am here to carry out the orders I receive.'

'A very proper reply, Station-Commander,' commented

The Outward Urge

the doctor, and went on waiting. He did not amplify, and she found the continuation thrown back on her.

'They tell me,' she observed, 'that we have something like seventy major missiles, with atomic war-heads. It has frequently been pointed out that the earlier the big blows fall, the more effective they are in destroying the enemy's potential – and in preventing retaliation. The aim, in fact, is the quick knock-out. But there our missiles still rest – unused even now.'

'Their use,' Troon pointed out again, 'is not for us here to decide. It is possible that the first intercontinental missiles did what was required – in which case it would simply be waste to launch these. It is not impossible, either, that if they are held in reserve there could be a point when our ability to continue the bombardment might be decisive.'

She shook her head.

'If the strategic targets have been destroyed, what is there left for decisive bombardment? These aren't weapons for use against armies in the field. What is worrying our personnel is, why weren't our weapons used – on the right kind of targets, at the right time?'

Troon shrugged.

'This is a pointless discussion, Ellen. Even if we were able to fire without orders, what should we aim at? We've no idea which targets have been destroyed, or which are only damaged. Indeed, for all we know, some of the target areas may now be occupied by our own people. If we had been needed, we should have had the orders.'

The doctor remained quiet for a full half minute, making up her mind. Then she said, forthrightly:

'I think you had better understand this, Michael. If there is not some use made of these missiles very soon, or if there is not some intelligible statement about them from H.Q., you are going to have a mutiny on your hands.'

The Moon

The Commander sat quite still on the corner of the desk, looking not at her, but towards the window. Presently:

'As bad as that?' he asked.

'Yes, Michael. About as bad as it can be, short of open rebellion.'

'Hm. I wonder what they think they'll get out of that.'

'They aren't thinking much at all. They're worried sick, frustrated, feeling desperate, and needing some kind – any kind – of action to relieve the tension.'

'So they'd like to unhorse me, and poop off major atomic missiles, just for the hell of it.'

She shook her head, looking at him unhappily.

'It's not exactly that, Michael. It's – oh dear, this is difficult – it's because a rumour has got round that they *should* have been sent off.'

She watched him as the implication came home. At length, he said, with icy calmness:

'I see. I am supposed to have the other Nelson touch – the blind eye?'

'Some of them say so. A lot of the rest are beginning to wonder.'

'There has to be a reason. Even a Command Officer must be supposed to have a motive for dereliction of duty amounting to high treason.'

'Of course, Michael.'

'Well, I'd better have it. What is it?'

Ellen took a deep breath.

'It's this. So long as we don't send those missiles we may be safe: once we do start sending them we'll probably bring down retaliation, either from the Russian Station, if it still exists, or from one of their satellites. Our nine medium missiles haven't been a serious matter – not serious enough to justify them into provoking us to use our heavies. But, if we *do* start to use the major ones, it will almost

The Outward Urge

certainly mean the end of this station. Your own view of the primary importance of the station is well known – you admitted it to me just now. . . . So, you see, a motive can be made to appear . . .

'The American Station has almost certainly gone; possibly the Russian, too. If we go as well, there will no longer be anyone on what you called the "threshold of the universe". *But*, if we were able somehow to ride out the war, we should be in sole possession of the moon, and still on the threshold . . . Shouldn't we ?'

'Yes. You make the motive quite uncomfortably clear,' he told her. 'But an ambition is not necessarily an obsession, you know.'

'This is a closed community, in a high state of nervous tension.'

He thought for some moments, then :

'Can you predict ? Will it produce a revolution, or a mass-rising ?' he asked her.

'A revolution,' she said, without hesitation. 'Your officers will arrest you, once they have plucked up the courage. That could take a day or two yet. It is a pretty grim step – especially when the C.O. happens to be a popular figure, too. . . .' She shrugged her shoulders.

'I must think,' he said.

He went round behind the desk and sat down, resting his elbows on it. The room became as quiet as the construction of the station permitted while he considered behind closed eyes. After several minutes he opened them.

'*If* they should arrest me,' he said, 'their next move must be to search the message files : (*a*) to justify themselves by finding evidence against me, and (*b*) to find out what the orders were, and whether they can still be carried out.

'When they discover that, except for three sets of three medium missiles, no launching orders have been received,

The Moon

there will be a panic. Such of my officers as may have been persuaded into this will be utterly shattered – you can't just apologize to your C.O. for arresting him as a traitor, and expect it to be left at that.

'There will be just one hope left, so someone more decisive than the rest will radio H.Q. that I have had a breakdown, or something of the kind, and request a repeat of all launching orders. When that brings nothing but a repetition of the same three sets of three, they'll be really sunk.

'Then, I should think, there will be a split. Some of them will have cold feet, and be for taking the consequences before matters get even worse; a number of men are bound to say "in for a penny, in for a pound", and want to launch the missiles anyway. Some will have swung back, and argue that if H.Q. wanted launchings they would have said so – so why risk a further act of wanton insubordination which will probably bring enemy reprisals, anyway.

'Even if good sense and cold feet were to win, and I should be released, I should have lost much of my authority and prestige, and there would be a very, very sticky situation all the way round.

'On the whole, I think it would be easier for everyone if I were to swallow my pride and discourage my arrest by anticipating their second move.'

He paused, contemplating the doctor.

'As you know, Ellen, it is not a habit of mine to reflect aloud in this manner. But I think it would do no harm if some idea of the probable results of my arrest were to filter round. Don't you agree?'

She nodded, without speaking. He got up from the desk.

'I shall now send for Sub-Commander Reeves – and I think we will have Sub-Commander Calmore as well – and explain to them with as little loss of face as possible that, the chances of war being what they are, and the chances of leakage now being nil, I am lifting security on messages received. This is being done in order that all senior officers may fully acquaint themselves with the situation, in readiness for any emergency.

'This should have enough deflationary effect to stop them from making that particular kind of fool of themselves, don't you think?'

'But won't they just say that you must have destroyed the relevant messages?' she objected.

'Oh, that one wouldn't do. There's service procedure. They will be able to compare my file with the Codes Section's files, and that with the Radio Section's log-book, and they'll find they all tie up.'

She went on studying him.

'I still don't understand why our missiles have not been launched,' she said.

'No? Well, perhaps all will be revealed to us one day. In the meantime – suppose we just go on obeying our orders. It's really much simpler.

'But I am extremely grateful to you, Ellen. I had not thought it had got so far, yet. Let's hope that tomorrow will show, if not a great change of feeling, at least a less awkward choice of scapegoat. And now, if you will excuse me, I will send for those two.'

As the door closed behind her, he continued to stare at it for fully a minute. Then he flipped over a switch, and requested the presence of his sub-commanders.

With the interview over, Troon allowed a few minutes for the officers to get clear. They had gone off looking a little winded, one carrying the message file, the other his signed authority of access to the code files, in a bemused way. Then, feeling the need for a change, he, too, left his room

The Moon

and made his way to the entrance-port. In the dressing-room the man on duty jumped to his feet and saluted.

'Carry on, Hughes,' Troon told him. 'I'm going outside for an hour or so.'

'Yes, sir,' said the man. He sat down and resumed work on the suit he was servicing.

Troon lifted his own scarlet pressure suit from its pegs, and inspected it carefully. Satisfied, he shed his uniform jacket and trousers, and got into it. He carried out the routine checks and test; finally, he switched on the radio, and got an acknowledgement from the girl at the main instrument desk. He told her that he would be available for urgent calls only. When he spoke again his voice reached the duty man from a loudspeaker on the wall. The man got up, and moved to the door of the smaller, two-man airlock.

'An hour, you said, sir?' he inquired.

'Make it an hour and ten minutes,' Troon told him.

'Yes, sir.' The man set the hand of the reminder-dial seventy minutes ahead of the clock. If the Station-Commander had not returned, or had failed to notify an extension by then, the rescue squad would automatically be summoned.

The duty man operated the lock, and presently Troon was outside; a vivid splash of colour in the monochrome landscape, the only moving thing in the whole wilderness. He set off southward with the curious, lilting moon-step which long service had made second nature.

At half a mile or so he paused, and made a show of inspecting one or two of the missile-pits there. They were, as they were intended to be, almost invisible. The top of each shaft had a cover of stiff fibre which matched the colour of the ground about it. A scatter of sand and stones on top made it difficult to detect, even at a few yards. He

The Outward Urge

pottered from one to another for a few minutes, and then stood looking back at the station.

It was dwarfed and made toy-like by the mountains behind it. The radar and radio towers, and the sun-bowls looking like huge artificial flowers on the top of their masts, gave a rough scale; but for them it would have been difficult to judge whether the station itself was the size of a half-inflated balloon, or half a puff-ball. It was hard to appreciate that the main body was a hundred and twenty yards in diameter at ground level until one looked at the corridors connecting it with the smaller storage-domes, and remembered that the roofs of those corridors were four feet above one's head.

Troon continued to regard it for some moments, then he turned round, pursued a zigzag course between the missile-pits, and when he was hidden from the station by a rocky outcrop, sat down. There he leaned back and, in such modified comfort as the suit allowed, contemplated the prospect dominated by the bright segment of Earth – and also the shape of the future in a world ruined by war.

All his life – and, for the matter of that, all his father's life, too – the possibility of such a war had lurked in the background. Sometimes it had seemed imminent, but there had been *rapprochements*; then again, it had seemed inevitable, but in one way or another it had been avoided. Again and again the tensions had increased and relaxed. There had been conferences, concessions, compromises, bluffs, crises, and occasional panic moves, but through them all the taper had somehow been kept at a safe distance from the touch-hole.

Three years ago, when he had once more, and certainly for the last time, managed to stave off 'grounding', he had felt an increased sense of imminence. It was difficult to be sure that the placidity of his spells on the moon did not

The Moon

give a distorted impression that life at home was becoming more febrile and exhausting each leave, but of one thing he was convinced – he had no intention of spending his retirement in one of the regions that grew tense with the jitters two or three times every year.

It was for that reason he had sold his house – the house that had been presented to his mother in tribute to the memory of his father – and moved his family four thousand miles to a new home in Jamaica.

Ridding himself of the house had been satisfactory in another way, too, for to him it had symbolized the superhuman obligation of living up to his father's legendary reputation; it had been a solidification of the shadows that his father had unwittingly cast over him since he was twelve years old.

Looking back on his life, it was only those years before he was twelve that appeared sunlit and halcyon. He, his mother, and his grandfather had then lived quietly and happily in a roomy cottage. They had their friends and neighbours; he had his own school friends in the village; beyond that small circle they had been, except for his grandfather's reputation as a classical scholar, unnoticed and unknown. And then, in the September of his thirteenth year, had come the break-up.

A man called Tallence had somehow stumbled across the story of Ticker Troon and the missile, and had applied to the authorities for the lifting of the security ban. After twelve years there was no good reason for silence – and, indeed, had been none for some time. Four Satellite Stations had for several years been known to be in position – the British one, two fair-sized Russian ones, and the huge American one. The existence of space-mines was no longer a secret, nor was the fact that all the stations now carried means to combat them. Tallence, therefore, had managed to carry his point and, presently, to produce his book.

It was a good book, and the publishers spared nothing on the publicity that launched it; the conveniently timed citation of a posthumous V.C. for Ticker Troon helped, too; and the book went straight into the epic class. It sold by the hundred thousands; it was seized upon by translators at once, and went into all languages save those allied with the Intransigent Sixth, where it was believed that the space-station was a Soviet invention. It was filmed, televised, digested, and strip-treated until, a year later, there was scarcely a man, woman, or child outside the Soviet Empire who did not know of Ticker Troon and his exploit.

For his son, it had been all very exciting at first. Suddenly to discover that one had a hero father, to be invited to big parties, to have news-writers and cameramen besieging, to take the seat of honour at a première, to be introduced on platforms, were great thrills. Soon, however, he had become awkwardly conscious of his ignorance, and of people's disappointment when their talk of space meant nothing to him. To overcome that, he had begun to read books on astronomy and spacework. In them he learnt that his grandfather had not been fully informative in teaching him that the Pleiades were the seven daughters of Atlas, that Venus emerged from the sea, that Orion was the great hunter who met his match in Diana. And as he read he too had seemed to hear 'the far gnat-voices cry, star to faint star across the sky'.

The excitement of being a public figure had soon worn off. The sense of being watched became distasteful. The feeling that he was expected to be exceptional weighed upon him at school, and only slightly less when he went up to Oxford. The house that his mother had accepted with a feeling of reluctant obligation never had the quality of home that there had been in the cottage. His mother seemed

The Moon

to be forever socially busy now; his new interests were not shared by his grandfather; it seemed impossible to remain unreminded for an hour that he was the son of Ticker Troon – and that was rather like finding one had Sir Francis Drake, Lord Nelson, or the National Gallery for a father.

His discovered fascination with the problems of space made it worse; as if a part of him had turned traitor and conspired to draw him away from his old interests, and deeper into his father's shadow. He tried hard to retain the belief that Phoebus Apollo was more interesting than Phoebus, the Eye of Heaven; that Mars, as the alias of the roughneck son of Zeus and Hera, had more significance than Mars, the nearest and potentially most attainable of the planets; that Aristotle, the Peripatetic, was of more importance than the crater on the moon that had been named after him, but in vain. An unquenchable curiosity had sprung alight in his mind, and presently he had been forced to admit that though his father's qualities might be beyond him, he had certainly inherited his one passionate interest. With that once decided, he had been willing to set about using his name to further it, and he had entered the Service.

He had, at first, used it quite diffidently. He did not seek publicity; that was not necessary, but neither did he shun it any longer. He avoided the cheaply sensational, but he was not unaware that more restrained publicity was gradually building him into a somebody in the public mind. When the press asked for his opinion on spatial questions, he gave it with careful consideration – and he was in a strong enough position to cause trouble over any misrepresentations. He adopted a deliberate policy, and, little by little, by the time he was twenty-five, he had built the space-hero's son into the ordinary man's oracle on space.

He did not do it without arousing jealousies, but his

popular position was solid, his discretion carefully judged. He was known to work hard, he saw to it that his service record was good, he knew that his opinions had started to carry weight.

Troon's first brush with the politicians had followed the announcement (a premature announcement, in point of fact) that the Russians were about to set up a Moon Station. The immediate effect of this was that the Americans, who had got into the habit of regarding the moon as a piece of U.S.-bespoken real estate that they would get around to developing when they were ready, were shocked into intense activity. The press wanted, as usual, to know Lieutenant Troon's views on the situation. He had them ready, and they made their first appearance in a responsible Sunday newspaper with an influential circulation.

He was well aware of the situation. A Moon Station was not a thing that could be set up for just a few million pounds. It could not but entail an expenditure that the government would be alarmed to contemplate, and he knew that the official policy would be to discourage any suggestion of a British Moon Station as a frivolous and profligate project, minimizing, or brushing aside, all arguments in its favour.

In his short article, Troon had mentioned the advantages to strategy and to science, but had dwelt chiefly upon prestige. Failure to establish such a station would be a turning point in British policy; it would amount to the first concrete confession that Britain was content to drop out of the van; that, in fact, it was now willing to admit itself as a second- or third-rate power. It would be public confirmation of the view, held in many circles for some time now, that the British had had their day, and were dwindling into their sunset; that all their greatness would soon lie with that of Greece, Rome, and Spain – in their past.

The Moon

Troon's first carpeting over the matter was by his C.O. He then trod a number of ascending carpets until he found himself facing a somewhat pompous Under-Secretary who began, as the rest had done, by pointing out that he had broken Service regulations by publishing an unapproved article, and then worked round by degrees to the suggestion that he might, upon reconsideration, find that a Moon Station had little strategic superiority to an armed Satellite Station, and that if the Americans and Russians did build them, they would be wasting material and money.

'Moreover, I am able to tell you confidentially,' the Under-Secretary had added, 'that this is also the view of the American authorities themselves.'

'Indeed, sir,' said Troon. 'In that case it seems odd that they should be doing it.'

'They would not be, I assure you, but for the Russians. Clearly, the moon cannot be left entirely to Russian exploitation. So, as the Americans can afford to do it, they are doing it in spite of their views on its worth. And since they are, it is not necessary for us to do so.'

'You think, sir, that it will do us no harm to be seen standing on American feet instead of on our own in this enterprise?'

'Young man,' said the Under-Secretary severely, 'there are many pretensions which are not worth the price they would exact. You have been unpatriotic enough to suggest in print that our sun is setting. I emphatically deny that. Nevertheless, it has to be admitted that whatever we have been, and whatever we may yet be, we are not, at present, one of the wealthier nations. We cannot afford such an extravagance for mere ostentation.'

'But if we do keep out of this, sir, our prestige cannot fail to suffer, whatever arguments we may advance. As for the American denial of strategic value, I have heard it before;

The Outward Urge

and I continue to regard it as wool-pulling. A Moon Station would be far less vulnerable, and could mount vastly greater fire power, than any Satellite Station.'

The Under-Secretary's manner had become cold.

'My information does not support that statement. Nor does the policy of the government. I must therefore request you ...'

Troon had heard him out politely and patiently. He knew, and he was sure that the Under-Secretary must know, too, that the damage already done to the declared policy was considerable. There would be a campaign for a Moon Station, certainly. Even if he were publicly to reverse his views, or even if he were to remain silent, the newspapers would enjoy tilting at those who had brought pressure to bear on him. He had only to behave circumspectly for a few weeks while the campaign gathered force, to refuse to give opinions where he had been ready to give them before, and perhaps look a little rueful in his silence. ... There would have been a campaign in some of the popular papers in any case; the main effect of his making his views known early was that in the public mind he appeared as the Moon Station's most important advocate.

In a few weeks, feeling among the electors had become clear enough to worry the government, and produce a rather more conciliatory tone. It was conceded that a British Moon Station *might* be considered, if the estimates were satisfactory. The prodigious size of the estimates which were produced, however, came as a shock which sharpened the divided opinions.

At this point, the Americans took a kindly hand. They had apparently changed their views on the value of Moon Stations, and, having done so, felt that it would be advantageous for the West to have two such stations to the rival's one. Accordingly, they offered to advance a part of the cost,

The Moon

and supply much of the equipment. It was a generous gesture.

'Good old Uncle Sam,' said Troon, when the offer was announced. 'Still the genial patron with two left feet.'

He was right. There was a considerable body of opinion to demand: 'Whose Moon Station is this supposed to be, anyway?'

Nevertheless, the number of noughts to the cost remained intimidating.

Presently there was a rumour in circulation that the wrong kind of thinking – to put it at its least slanderous – was going on at high levels, and that there was actually in existence a scheme by which a station could be established at a cost very considerably under half the present estimates; and that Troon (you know, son of Ticker Troon) thought well of it.

Troon had waited, quietly.

Presently, he found himself again invited to high places. He was modestly surprised, and could not think how the proposal came to be connected with his name but, as a matter of fact, well, yes; he did happen to have seen a scheme. ... Oh no, it was quite an error to think it had anything to do with him, a complete misunderstanding. The idea had been worked out by a man called Flanderys. It certainly had some interesting points. Yes, he did know Flanderys slightly. Yes, he was sure that Flanderys would be glad to explain his ideas. ...

The American and Russian expeditions seemed, in so far as their claims had ever been sorted out, to have arrived on the moon simultaneously; the former landing in Copernicus, the latter in Ptolemy – both claiming priority, and both consequently announcing their annexation of the entire territory of the moon. Experience with the Satellite Stations had already shown that any romantic ideas of a *pax coelestis* should be abandoned but, as each expedition was highly vulnerable, both concerned themselves primarily with tunnelling into the rock in order to establish strongholds from which they would be able to dispute their rights with greater confidence.

Some six months later, the smaller British expedition set down in the crater of Archimedes, with the Russian six hundred miles away beyond the Apennine Mountains to the south, and the American four hundred miles or so to the north-east. There, in contrast with their intensively burrowing neighbours, they proceeded to establish themselves on the surface. They had, it was true, one drilling-machine, but this, compared with the huge tunnelling engines of the others that had cost a good many times their weight in uranium to transport, was a mere toy which they employed in sinking a series of six-foot diameter pits.

The Flanderys Dome, essentially a modification of Domes used in the Arctic for some years, was a simple affair to erect. It was spread out on a levelled part of the crater floor, coupled with hoses, and left to inflate. With only the light gravity of the moon weighing down its fabric, the outer casing was fully shaped at a pressure of eight pounds (Earth) per square inch, at fifteen it was perfectly taut. Then the contents of the various rockets and containers went into it through the airlocks, or the annuli. The air regenerating plants were started up, the temperature controls coupled, and the work of building the station inside the dome could begin.

The Americans, Troon recalled, had been interested. They reckoned it quite an idea for use on a moon where there did not happen to be any Russians about; but on one where there were, they thought it plain nuts, and said so. The Russians themselves, he remembered with a smile, had been bewildered. A flimsy contrivance that could be completely

The Moon

wrecked by a single, old-fashioned H.E. shell was in their opinion utter madness, and a sitting temptation. They did not, however, yield to the temptation since that would almost certainly precipitate untimely action by the Americans. Nevertheless, the presumption of a declining Power in arriving to settle itself blandly and unprotected in the open while two great Powers were competing to tunnel themselves hundreds of feet into the rock was a curious piece of effrontery. Even a less suspicious mind than the Russian could well have felt that there was something here that was not meeting the eye. They instructed their agents to investigate.

The investigation took a little time, but presently the solution forthcame – an inconvenient clarification. As had been assumed, the pits that the British had been busily drilling at the same time that they built their station into the Dome were missile-shafts. This was similar to the work being done by the other two parties themselves – except that where the Americans also used pits, the Russians favoured launching ramps. The more disturbing aspect of it came to light later.

The British system of control, it appeared, was to use a main computing-engine to direct the aim and setting of any missile. Once the missile had been launched, it was kept on course by its own computer and servo systems. The main computer was, unlike the rest of the station, protected in a chamber drilled to a considerable depth. One of its more interesting features was that in certain conditions it was capable of automatically computing for, and dispatching, missiles until all were gone. A quite simple punched-card system was used in conjunction with a chronometer; each card being related to a selected target. One of the conditions which would cause this pack of cards to be fed to the computer was a drop in the station's air-pressure. Fifteen pounds per square inch was its normal, and there was allowance for reasonable variation. Should the Dome be so unfortunate, however, as to suffer a misfortune sufficient to reduce the air-pressure to seven pounds, the missile-dispatching mechanism would automatically go into action.

All things considered, it appeared highly desirable from the Russian point of view that the Flanderys Dome should not suffer any such misadventure.

During the years that had intervened between the establishment of the station and his succeeding to command of it, Troon had taken part in a number of expeditions. Some, such as that which had visited the Apennines, had consisted of fourteen or fifteen men travelling with their supplies on tractors, surveying, mapping, photographing as they went; spending their sleeping periods in small Flanderys Domes holding several men, where they could remove their pressure-suits to eat and attain some degree of comfort. Others, ranging further, were two-, three-, or four-man trips on jet-borne platforms. Tractor operations were limited by the huge cracks which radiated from the crater to form impassable obstacles, many of them more than a hundred miles in length and a mile wide. The cracks were at most times awesome clefts of unknown, inky depth. Only when the sun was overhead, or shining up their length, was one able to see the rocky debris which choked them several miles below, and it was only at such times that the geologists, turned selenologists, were able to take their jet-platforms down, and make their brief notes while the light lasted.

Troon, who had rapidly become something of a selenologist himself, had nursed from the time of the landing an ambition to see and record something of the moon's other side. According to rumour, the Russians had, within a year of their arrival, sent an ill-fated expedition there, but the

The Moon

truth or otherwise of the report remained hidden by the usual Slav passion for secrecy. It was one of Troon's regrets that exploration would have to wait on further development of the jet-platforms, but there was no reason to think that the invisible side held any surprises; photographs taken from circling rockets showed no more than a different pattern of the same pieces – mountains, 'seas', and craters innumerable.

The regret that exploration must fall to someone else was no more than minor; most of what he had wanted to do, he had done. The establishment of the Moon Station was the end to which he had worked, manoeuvred, and contrived. He had given Flanderys the idea of the Dome, and helped him to work it out; and, when that looked like being rejected for its vulnerability, he had briefed another friend to produce the solution of automatic reprisals which they had called Project Stalemate. It was better, he had thought then and still thought, that the affair should appear to be a composite achievement rather than a one-man show. He was satisfied with his work.

He had almost reconciled himself to handing over the command in another eight months with the thought that the station's future was secure, for, however much it might be grudged as a charge on the armed forces, the discovery of rare elements had given it practical importance, the astronomers attached great value to the station, and the medical profession, too, had found it useful for special studies.

But now there had come this war, and he was wondering whether that might mean the end of all the Moon Stations. If this one survived, would there be the wealth, or even the technical means, left to sustain it when the destruction was finished? Was it not very likely that everybody would be too busy trying simply to survive in a shattered world to concern themselves with such exotic matters as the conquest of space ...?

Well, there was nothing he could do about that – nothing but wait and see what the outcome was, and be ready to seize any opportunity that showed.

And it was still possible that there might be no one left on the moon by the time it was over. The signs were that the two giants had felled one another already. One could do no more than hope that the threat of Project Stalemate would continue to ward off attack by the Russian Satellite Stations – if they were still in working order.... After all, the descent of some seventy fission and fission-fusion bombs on one's country would seem, even though that country was spread over one-sixth of the habitable globe, to be a heavy price to pay for the destruction of one small Moon Station ... Yes, given luck, and some sense of relative values in the enemy's mind, the British Moon Station still had quite a chance of survival....

Troon got up, and walked out from behind the rock. He stood for some moments, a lone scarlet figure in the black and white desert, looking at his Moon Station. Then, picking his path carefully between the missile-pits, he made his unhurried way back to it.

At the end of dinner he asked if he might have the pleasure of the doctor's company at coffee in his office. Looking at her over the rim of his cup, he said:

'It would seem to have worked.'

She regarded him quizzically through her cigarette smoke.

'Yes, indeed,' she agreed. 'Like a very hungry bacteriophage. I felt as if I were watching a film speeded up to twice natural pace.' She paused, and then added: 'Of course, I am not familiar with the usual reactions of Commanding

The Moon

Officers who have been suspected of treason and stood in some danger of lynching, but one would not have been surprised at a little more – er – perturbation....'

Troon grinned.

'A bit short on self-respect?' He shook his head. 'This is a funny place, Ellen. When you have been here a little longer your own sense of values will seem a little less settled.'

'I have suspected that already.'

'But you still need to get the measure of it. My immediate predecessor once said: "When I am on this singularly unheavenly cinder, I make it an invariable rule to assume that the emotional content of any situation is seventy-five per cent above par." I don't know how he arrived at the seventy-five, but the principle is entirely right. You know, you yourself weren't far off sharing the general opinion this morning – it gave you a sense of the dramatic, an angle for the feeling of tension, and helped to relieve the boredom of the place. You would not have felt like that at home; and I should not have behaved as I did, at home; but here, the occasions for standing firm, and for bending, are different. Technically, I am the C.O., with all the authority of the Crown behind me, and because of that we preserve certain forms; in practice, my job is more like a patriarch's. Sometimes rank and regulations have to be invoked; but we find it better to use them as little as we can.'

'I have noticed that, too,' she agreed.

'We realized when we came here that there would be particular problems, but we could not foresee all of them. We realized that we'd need men able to adapt to life in a small community, and because they would be restricted almost all the time to the station, we had them vetted for claustrophobic tendencies, too. But it did not occur to anyone that, out here, they would have to contend with

73

claustrophobia and agoraphobia at the same time. Yet it is so; we are shut in, in a vast emptiness – it made a pretty grim mental conflict for a lot of them, and morale went down and down. After a year of it the first Station-Commander began to battle for an establishment of women clerks, orderlies, and cooks. His report was quite dramatically eloquent. "If this station," he wrote, "is required to keep to its present establishment then, in my considered opinion, a complete collapse of morale will follow in a short time. It is of the utmost importance that we take all practical steps which will help to give it the character of a normal human community. Any measures that will keep this wilderness from howling in the men's minds, and the horrors of eternity from frost-biting their souls, should be employed without delay." Good Lyceum stuff, that, but true, all the same. There was a great deal of misgiving at home – but no lack of women volunteers; and when they did come, most of them turned out to be more adaptable than the men. And then, of course, the patriarchal aspect of the C.O.'s job came still more to the fore. It is no sort of a place for a disciplinarian to build up his ego; the best that can be done is to keep it working as harmoniously as possible.

'I have been here long enough to take its pulse fairly well as a rule, but this time I slipped up. Now, I don't want that to happen again, so I'd be glad of your further help to see that it doesn't. We've dislodged this particular source of trouble, but the causes are still there; the frustrations are still buzzing about, and soon they are going to find a new place to swarm. I want the news early, the moment they look as if they have found it. Can I rely on you for that?'

'But, seeing that the cause – the immediate cause, that is – is H.Q.'s failure to use us, I don't see that there is anything here for them to concentrate the frustration on.'

The Moon

'Nor do I. But since they cannot reach the high-brass back home, they will find something or other to sublimate it on, believe me.'

'Very well, I'll be your ear to the ground. But I still don't understand. Why – why *doesn't* H.Q. use these missiles? We know we should be plastered, wiped out, in an attempt to put the main computer out of action. But most of the men are past caring about that. They have reached a sort of swashbuckling, *Götterdämmerung* state of mind by now. They reckon that their families, their homes, and their towns must have gone, so they are saying: "What the hell matters now?" There is still just a hope that we are being reserved for a final, smashing blow, but when that goes, I think they'll try to fire them themselves.'

Troon thought a little, then he said:

'I think we have passed the peak of likelihood of desperate action. Now that they are sure that no firing orders were received, they must most of them swing over to the proposition that we are being conserved for some decisive moment – with the corollary that if our missiles are not available when they are called for, the whole strategy of a campaign could be wrecked. After all, could it not come to the point where the last man who still has ammunition holds the field? For all we can tell, we may at this very moment be representing a threat which dominates the whole situation. Someone could be saying: "Unconditional surrender *now*. Or we'll bomb you again from the moon." If so, we are rather an emphatic example of "they also serve..."'

'Yes,' she said, after reflection. 'I think that *must* be the intention. What other reason could there be?'

Troon looked thoughtfully after her as she left. Her predecessor would have spread such a theory, offered as her own, all round the station in half an hour. He was not quite

The Outward Urge

sure yet how much Ellen talked, and who listened to her. However, that would soon reveal itself. In the meantime he turned to the day's reports, and spent an hour filling in the Station's Log, and his own private log.

Before leaving the office, he went over to the window again. The scene had not changed greatly since 'morning'. The crater floor was still harsh in the sunlight of the long lunar day. The cut-out mountains looked just the same, just the same as they had for ten million years. The nacreous Earth had moved only a few degrees, and still hung with the night-line half across her face, and the other half veiled.

Presently he sighed, and turned towards the door of his sleeping cabin....

The jangle of the bedside telephone woke Troon abruptly. He had the handpiece to his ear before his eyes were well open.

'Radar Watch here, sir,' said a voice, with a tinge of excitement behind it. 'Two ufos observed approaching south-east by south. Height one thousand; estimated speed under one hundred.'

'Two *what*?' inquired Troon, collecting his wits.

'Unidentified flying objects, sir.'

He grunted. It was so long since he had encountered the term that he had all but forgotten it.

'You mean jet-platforms?' he suggested.

'Possibly, sir.' The voice sounded a little hurt.

'You've warned the guard?'

'Yes, sir. They're in the lock now.'

'Good. How far off are these – ere – ufos?'

'Approximately forty miles now.'

'Right. Pick them up televisually as soon as possible, and let me know. Tell switchboard to cut me in on the guard's link right away.'

The Moon

Troon put down the telephone, and threw back the bedcovers. He had barely put a foot on the floor when there was a sound of voices in his office next door. One, more authoritative than the rest, cut across the babble.

'Zero, boys. Open her up.'

Troon, still in his pyjamas, went through to his office and approached his desk. From the wallspeaker came the sound of breathing, and the creak of gear as the men left the lock. A voice said:

'Damned if I can see any bloody ufos. Can you, Sarge?'

'*That*,' said the sergeant's voice patiently, 'is south-east by south, my lad.'

'Okay. But I still can't see a bloody ufo. If you –'

'Sergeant Witley,' said Troon, into the microphone. A hush fell over the party.

'Yes, sir.'

'How many are you?'

'Six men with me, sir. Six more following.'

'Arms?'

'Light machine-gun and six bombs, each man, sir. Two rocket-tubes for the party.'

'That'll do. Ever used a gun on the moon, Sergeant?'

'No, sir.' There was a touch of reproof in the man's voice, but one did not waste ammunition that had cost several pounds a round to bring in. Troon said:

'Put your sights right down. For practical purposes there is no trajectory. If you do have to shoot, try to get your back against a rock; if you can't do that, lie down. Do *not* try to fire from a standing position. If you haven't learnt the trick of it, you'll go into half a dozen back somersaults with the first burst. All of you got that?'

There were murmured acknowledgements.

'I don't for a moment suppose it will be necessary to shoot,' Troon continued, 'but be ready. You will not initiate hostilities, but at any sign of a hostile act you, Sergeant, will reply instantly, and your men will give you support. No one else will act on his own. Is that clear?'

'Yes, sir.'

'Good. Carry on now, Sergeant Witley.'

To a background sound of the sergeant making his dispositions, Troon hurried into his clothes. He was almost dressed when the same voice as before complained:

'Still I don't see no bloody – yes, I do, though, by God! Something just caught the light to the right of old Mammoth Tooth, see . . . ?'

At the same moment the telephone rang. Troon picked it up.

'Got the telly on them now, sir. Two platforms. Four men on one, five on the other. Scarcely any gear with them. Wearing Russian-type suits. Headed straight this way.'

'Any weapons?'

'None visible, sir.'

'Very well. Inform the guard.'

He hung up, and listened to the sergeant receiving and acknowledging the message, while he finished dressing. Then he picked up the telephone again to tell the switchboard:

'Inform the W.O.'s mess that I shall observe from there. And switch the guard link through to there right away.'

He glanced at the looking-glass, picked up his cap, and left his quarters, with an air of purpose, but carefully unhurried.

When he arrived at the W.O.'s mess on the south-east side, the two platforms were already visible as shining specks picked out by the sunlight against the spangled black sky. His officers arrived at almost the same moment and stood beside him, watching the specks grow larger. Presently, in spite of the distance the clear airlessness made it possible to

The Moon

see the platforms themselves, the pinkish-white haze of the jets supporting them, and the clusters of brightly coloured space-suits upon them. Troon did not try to judge the distance; in his opinion, nothing less precise than a range-finder was any use on the moon. He clicked on the hand mike.

'Sergeant Witley,' he instructed, 'extend your men in a semi-circle, and detail one of them to signal the platforms down within it. Control, cut my guard-link now, but leave me linked to you.'

'Guard-link cut, sir.'

'Is your standby with you?'

'Yes, sir.'

'Tell her to search for the Russian intercom wave-length. It's something a little shorter than ours as a rule. When she finds it, she is to hold it until further notice. Does she speak Russian?'

'Yes, sir.'

'Good. She is to report at once if there is any suggestion of hostile intention in their talk. Cut me in on the guard-link again now.'

The two platforms continued smoothly towards them, dropping on a long slant as they came. The sergeant's men were prone, with their guns aimed. They were deployed in a wide crescent. In the middle of it stood a lone figure in a suit of vivid magenta, his gun slung, while he beckoned the platforms in with both arms. The platforms slowed to a stop a dozen yards short of the signaller, at a height of some ten feet. Then, with their jets blowing dust and grit away from under them, they sank gently down. As they landed, the space-suited figures on them let go of their holds, and showed empty hands.

'One of them is asking for you, sir, in English,' Control told him.

The Outward Urge

'Cut him in,' Troon instructed.

A voice with a slight foreign accent, and a trace of American influence, said:

'Commander Troon, please allow me to introduce myself. General Alexei Goudenkovitch Budorieff, of the Red Army. I had the honour to command the Moon Station of the U.S.S.R.'

'Commander Troon speaking, General. Did I understand you to say that you *had* that honour?'

He gazed out of the window at the platforms, trying to identify the speaker. There was something in the stance of a man in a searing orange suit that seemed to single him out.

'Yes, Commander. The Soviet Moon Station ceased to exist several earth-days ago. I have brought my men to you because we are – very hungry.'

It took a moment for the full implication to register, and then Troon was not quite sure.

'You mean you have brought *all* your men, General?'

'All that are left, Commander.'

Troon stared out at the little group of nine men in their vivid pressure-suits. The latest Intelligence Report, he recalled, had given the full complement of the Russian Station as three hundred and fifty-six. He said:

'Please come in, General. Sergeant Witley, escort the General and his men to the airlock.'

The General gazed round at the officers assembled in their mess. Both he and his aide beside him were looking a great deal better for two large meals separated by ten hours of sleep. The lines of hunger and fatigue had left his face, though signs of strain remained.

'Gentlemen,' he said, 'I have decided to give you an account of the action at the Moon Station of the U.S.S.R. while it is fresh in my mind, for several reasons. One is that

The Moon

I consider it a piece for the history books – and for the military experts, too. Another is that, although it appears to have brought the campaign in this theatre to a close, the war still continues, and none of us can tell what may happen to him yet. With this in mind, your Commander has pointed out that knowledge carried in a number of heads has a better chance of survival than if it is restricted to two or three, and suggested that I, who am in a better position to give the account than anyone else, should speak to you collectively. This I am not only honoured, but glad, to do, for it seems to me important that it should be known that our station fell to a new technique of warfare – an attack by dead men.'

He paused to regard the faces about him, and then went on:

'What you call in English the booby-trap – something which is set to operate after a man has left it, or is dead; a kind of blind vengeance by which he hopes to do some damage still – that is nothing new; it is, one would imagine, as old as war itself. But a means by which dead men can not only launch, but can press home an attack – that, I think, is new indeed. Nor do I yet see where such a development may lead.'

He paused again, and remained so long looking at the table in front of him that some of his audience fidgeted. The movement caught his attention, and he looked up.

'I will start by saying that, to the best of my knowledge, all life that still exists upon the Moon is now gathered here, in your Dome.

'Now, how did this come about? You are no doubt aware in outline of the first stages. We and the American Station opened our bombardments simultaneously. Neither of us attacked the other. Our orders were to disregard the American Station, and give priority to launching our earth-bound

The Outward Urge

missiles. I have no doubt that their orders were similarly to disregard us. This situation persisted until, of our heavy missiles, only the strategic reserve remained. It might well have continued longer had not the Americans, with a light missile, destroyed our incoming supply-rocket. Upon this, I requested, and received, permission to attack the American Station, for we had a second supply-rocket already on the way, and hoped to save it from the same fate.

'As you know, the use of heavy, ground-to-ground missiles is not practicable here, nor would an attempt to use our small reserve for such a purpose have been permitted. We therefore retaliated with light missiles on high-angle setting to clear the mountains round the Copernicus crater. Again as you will know, the low gravity here gives a wide margin of error for such an attempt, and our missiles were ineffective. The Americans attempted to reply with similar missiles, and they, too, were highly inaccurate. There was slight damage to one of our launching ramps, but no more.

'Then one of our Satellite Stations which chanced to be in a favourable position dispatched two heavy missiles. The first they reported as being two miles off target; for the second, they claimed a direct hit. This would seem to be a valid claim, for the American Station ceased at once to communicate, and has shown no sign of life since.

'A reprisal attack on our own station from the American Satellite was to be expected, and it came in the form of one heavy missile which landed within a mile of us. Our chief damage was fractures in the walls of the upper chambers, causing a considerable air-leakage. We had to close them off with bulkheads while we sent men in space-suits to caulk the larger fissures and spray the walls and roofs with plastic sealing compound. The area of damage was extensive, and the work was hampered by falls from the roof, so that I decided to remain incommunicado, in the hope of attracting

The Moon

no more missiles until we had stopped the leaks. It was to be hoped, too, that now the Satellites had been brought into the action ours might succeed in crippling the American with their wasps by the time we had made good.'

'Wasps?' somebody interrupted.

'You haven't heard of them? I'm surprised. However, it can do no harm now. They are very small missiles, used in a spread-out flock. A Satellite can easily meet one, or several, ordinary missiles with counter-missiles and explode them at a safe distance, but with missiles that come to the attack like a shoal of fish, defence is difficult, and some will always get through – or so it is claimed.'

'And did they, General?' Troon asked. He gave no indication of knowing that the British Satellite which his father had helped to construct, was disabled, and nothing had been heard from the American Satellite since the second day of hostilities.

The General shook his head.

'I cannot say. By the time we had our leaks repaired and our mast up again, there was a message from H.Q. saying that it had lost touch with our Satellites....'

His earlier formality had eased, and he went on more easily, as a man telling his story.

'We thought then that we had, as you say, come through. But it was not yet certain that there would be no further attack, or that more cracks in the roof might not open, so we kept our suits handy. That was very fortunate for some of us.

'Five earth-days ago – that is four whole days after the American Station was hit – the man on television watch thought he caught a glimpse of something moving among the rocks on the crater floor to the north of us. It seemed improbable, but he held the masthead scanner on the area and presently he caught another movement – something swiftly crossing a gap between two rocks – and he reported it. The Duty-Officer watched, too, and soon he also caught a snatch of movement, but it occurred too rapidly for him to be sure what it was. They switched in a telephoto lens, but it reduced the field of view, and showed them nothing but rocks, so they went back to the normal lens just in time to see what looked like a smooth rock appear from the cover of one ordinary jagged rock and slither behind another. At this point the Duty-Officer reported to me, and I went down to join them in the main control-chamber.

'Viewing conditions were difficult on account of the cross-light – the dawn had only begun the previous Earth-day, so that the long shadows gave dark bars of cover, but anything that moved in the sunlight also threw a long shadow to catch the eye. After a few minutes' watching I had to agree that something, though I could not distinguish what, was moving out there, apparently in sharp, sudden dashes. Once, it paused in the open. We hurriedly cut in the telephoto lens again, but before we could focus, the thing had flashed away, and become invisible in a dark patch.

'We alerted the guard to stand by with rocket-tubes, and went on watching. The thing kept on dodging about, suddenly shooting out of a black shadow, or from behind a rock, and vanishing again. There was no doubt that it was gradually coming closer, but it seemed in no hurry to reach us.

'Somebody said: "I think there must be two of them." The appearances and disappearances were so erratic that we could not be sure. We tried radar on it, but at that angle and among so much broken rock, it was practically useless. We could only wait for the thing to reach more open ground, and show itself more clearly.

'Then there was report from the guard of another moving object, somewhat further west. We turned the scanner

The Moon

that way, and observed that there was indeed a similar something there that dodged about among the rocks and shadows in the same, unidentifiable way.

'Over an hour went by before the first of them reached the more open ground at a range of eleven kilometres from us. But even then it was some time before we could get a real idea of it – for it was too small on the normal lens to show detail, and too erratic for the telephoto to follow it. Before long, however, there were three of the things all skirmishing wildly about the crater floor with sudden rushes forward, sideways, any direction, even back, and never staying still long enough for us to make them out clearly in the crosslight.

'If our armament had included short-range bombardment missiles, we should have used them at the first sighting, but they were not a weapon that had seemed reasonable equipment for a Moon Station, and we could only wait for the things to come within practicable range of the portable rocket-tubes.

'Meanwhile they continued to dash hither and thither zigzagging madly about the crater floor. It was uncanny. They made us think of huge spiders rushing back and forth, but they never froze as spiders do; their pauses were no more than momentary, and then they were off again; and one never could tell which way it would be. They must have been travelling quite thirty or forty metres to make an advance of one metre, and they were in an extended line so that we could only get one, or perhaps for a moment, two of them, on the screen at the same time.

'However, during the time it took them to cover the next two kilos we were able to get better views and impressions of them. In appearance they were simple. Take an egg, pull it out to double its length, and that is the shape of the body. Put long axles through it near the ends, and fasten

The Outward Urge

tall, wide-tyred wheels on them – tall enough to give it a good ground clearance. Mount the wheels so that they have a hundred and eighty degrees of traverse – that is, so that the treads can be turned parallel with the lines of the axle, whether the wheels themselves are before or behind the axle. And you have this machine. It can move in any direction – or spin in one spot, if you want it to. Not, perhaps, very difficult once you have thought of the idea. Give it a motor in each wheel, and an electronic control to keep it from hitting obstacles. That is not very difficult, either.

'What is not so clear is how you direct it. It was not, very clearly, by dead reckoning. We thought it might be responding to our radio, or to the rotation of our radar scanner, or to the movements of our television pick-up, but we tested all those, and even switched off our screen for some minutes, but the guard outside reported no effect. Nor was it detecting and seeking any of our electric motors; we stopped every one of them for a full minute, without any result. It was just possible that the things were picking up an emanation from our power-pile, but that was well shielded, and we already had decoy radiators to deflect any missiles that might try that. I myself think it probable that they were able to detect, and to respond to, the inevitable slight rise of temperature in the station area. If so, there was nothing we could have done about it.'

The General shrugged, shook his head, and frowned. He went on:

'What we faced, in essence, was a seeking missile on wheels. Not difficult to construct, though scarcely worth attempting for use in a simple form – too easy a target for the defence. So what those Americans had done, the frightening thing they had done, was to introduce a random element. You see what I mean? They had put in this random stage, and somehow filtered the control through it. . . .'

The Moon

He thought again for a moment.

'Machines do not live, so they cannot be intelligent. Nevertheless, it is in the nature of machines to be logical. The conception of an illogical machine seems to be a contradiction in terms. If you deliberately produce such a thing, what have you? Something that never existed in nature. Something alien. What you have done is to produce madness without mind. You have made unreason animate, and set it loose. That is a very frightening thing to think about....

'But here, among these not-quite-machines that were scuttering about the crater floor like water-boatmen on a pond, there was a controlling thread of ultimate purpose running through the artificial madness. Their immediate actions were unpredictable, insane, but their final intention was just as sure as the bomb that each was carrying in its metal belly. Think of a maniac, a gibbering idiot, with one single continuing thread of intention – to murder....

'That is what those machines were. And they kept on coming with short, or very short, or not so short crazy rushes. They darted and dodged forward, sideways, backwards, obliquely, straight, or in a curve; one never knew which would be next – only that, after a dozen moves, they would be just a little closer.

'Our rocket men opened fire at about five kilos. A sheer waste of course; one could as well have hoped to hit a fly on the wing with a peashooter. Mines might have stopped them – if they did not have detectors – but who would have sanctioned the use of valuable rocket-space to bring mines to the moon? All our men could do was to hope for a lucky shot. Occasionally one of them would be hidden for a moment or two by the burst of an explosion, but it always reappeared out of the dust, dodging as crazily as ever. Our eyes and heads ached with the strain of trying to follow them on the screen, and to detect some pattern in their movements – I'm sure myself that no pattern existed.

'At three kilos the men were doing no better with their shooting, and were starting to show signs of panic. I decided that at two kilos we would withdraw the men and get them below.

'The things kept on coming, as madly as ever. I tell you, I have never seen anything that frightened me more. There was the dervish-like quality of the random madness, and yet the known deadly purpose. And all the time there was the suggestion of huge, scuttering insects so that it was difficult not to think of them as being in some alien way alive ...

'Some of the rocket bursts did succeeed in peppering them with fragments now and then, but they were not harmed. As they approached the two-kilo line I told Colonel Zinochek, here, to withdraw the patrol. He picked up the microphone to speak, and at that moment one of the things hit a rocket bomb. We saw it run right into the bomb.

'The explosion threw it off the ground, and it came down on its back. The diameter of the wheels was large enough to allow it to run upside down. It actually began to do so, but then there was a great glare, and the screen went blank.

'Even at our depth the floor of the chamber lifted under us, and cracks ran up two of the walls.

'I switched on the general address system. It was still live, but I could not tell how much of the station it was reaching. I gave orders for everyone to put on space-suits, and stand by for further instructions.

'One could hope that the explosion of one machine might have set off the others, but we could not tell. They might have been shielded at the moment, or, even if they were not, either, or both, of them might have survived. Without air there is not the usual kind of blast and pressure-wave; there is flying debris, of course, but what else? So

The Moon

little work has been done on the precise effects of explosions here. Our mast had gone again, so that we were without radar or television. We had no means of telling whether the danger was over, or whether the machines were still scurrying about the crater floor like mad spiders; still working closer . . .

'If they were, we reckoned that it should take them about thirty-five minutes to reach us, at their former rate.

'No half-hour in my life has been as long as that one. Once we had our helmets on, and the intercoms were working, we did our best to learn what the damage was. It appeared to be fairly extensive in the upper levels, for there were few replies from there. I ordered all who could to make their way down to the lowest levels, and to stay there.

'Then there was absolutely nothing we could do but wait . . . and wait . . . Wondering if the things were indeed still skirmishing outside, and watching the minute-hand crawl round. . . .

'It took them – or it – exactly thirty-one minutes. . . .

'The whole place bounced, and threw me off my feet. I had a glimpse of cracks opening in the roof and walls, then the light went out, and something fell on me. . . .

'I don't need to go into details about the rest. Four of us in the control-chamber were left alive, and five in the level immediately above. None of us would have survived had the rock had earth-weight – nor should we have been able to shift it to clear a way to the emergency exit.

'Even so, it took us four Earth-days to dig our way through the collapsed passages. All the station's air was gone, of course, and we had to do it on dead men's air-bottles, and emergency rations – as long as the rations lasted – and with only one two-man inflatable chamber between us to eat in.

'The emergency exit was, of course, at some distance

from the main entrance, but even so, a part of the roof of the terminal chamber had fallen in and wrecked one of the platforms there; fortunately the other two were scarcely damaged. The outer doors of the airlock were at the base of a cliff, and though the cliff itself had been a shield from the direct force of the explosion, a quantity of debris had fallen in front of the doors so that we had to blast them open. That gave us a big enough opening to sail the platforms through, and avoid any radio-active contamination – and, I think, by reason of the airlock's position, any serious exposure to radiation ourselves.'

He looked round the group of officers.

'It has been chivalrous of you, gentlemen, to take us in. Let me, in return, assure you that we have no intention of making ourselves a liability. On the contrary. There is a large food store in our station. If the cisterns have remained intact, there is water; also, there are air regeneration supplies. But we need drilling gear to get at these things. If, when my men are rested, you can let us have the necessary gear, we shall be able to add very considerably to your reserves here.'

He turned to the window, and looked at the shining segment of Earth.

' – And that may be as well, for I have a feeling that we may be going to need all the supplies we can collect.'

When the meeting was broken up, Troon took the General and his aide along to his own office. He let them seat themselves and light cigarettes before he said:

'As you will understand, General, we are not equipped here to deal with prisoners of war. I do not know your men. Our station is vulnerable. What guarantees can you give against sabotage?'

'Sabotage!' exclaimed the General. 'Why should there be sabotage? My men are all perfectly sane, I assure you.

The Moon

They are as well aware as I am that if anything should happen to this station it must be the end of all of us.'

'But might there not be one – well, let us call him a selflessly patriotic man – who might consider it his duty to wreck this station, even at the cost of his own life?'

'I think not. My command was staffed by picked, intelligent men. They are well aware that no one is going to *win* this war now. So that the object has become to survive it.'

'But, General, are you not overlooking the fact that we, here, are still a fighting unit – the only one left in this theatre of war.'

The General's eyebrows rose a little. He pondered Troon for a moment, and then smiled slightly.

'I see. I have been a little puzzled. Your officers are still under that impression?'

Troon leaned forward to tap his cigarette ash into a tray.

'Perhaps I don't quite understand you, General.'

'Don't you, Commander? I am speaking of your value as a fighting unit.'

Their eyes met steadily for some seconds. Troon shrugged.

'How high would *you* place our value as a fighting unit, General?'

General Budorieff shook his head gently.

'Not very high, I am afraid, Commander,' he said, and then, with a touch of apology in his manner, continued: 'Before the last attack on our station you had dispatched nine medium missiles. I do not know whether you have fired any more since then, therefore the total striking power at your disposal may be either three medium missiles – or none at all.'

Troon turned, and looked out of the window towards the camouflaged missile-pits. His voice shook a little as he asked:

91

The Outward Urge

'May I inquire how long you have known this General?'

Gently the General said:

'About six months.'

Troon put his hand over his eyes. For a minute or two no one spoke. At length the General said:

'Will you permit me to extend my sincere congratulations, Commander Troon? You must have played it magnificently.'

Troon, looking up, saw that he was genuine.

'I shall have to tell them now,' he said. 'It's going to hurt their pride. They thought of everything but that.'

'It would, I think, be better to tell them now,' agreed Budorieff, 'but it is not necessary for them to know that *we* knew.'

'Thank you, General. That will at least do something to diminish the farcical element for them.'

'Do not take it too hard, Commander. Bluff and counter-bluff are, after all, an important part of strategy – and to have maintained such a bluff as that for almost twenty years is, if I may say so, masterly. I have been told that our people simply refused to believe our agents' first reports on it.

'Besides, what was our chief purpose here – yours, mine, and the Americans? Not to *make* war. We were a threat which, it was hoped, would help to *prevent* war – and one fancies that all of us here did do something to postpone it. Once fighting was allowed to start, it could make really very little difference whether our missiles were added to the general destruction or not. We have all known in our hearts that this war, if it should come, would not be a kind that anyone could win.

'For my part, I was greatly relieved when I received this report on your armament. The thought that I might one day be required to destroy your quite defenceless station

The Moon

was not pleasant. And consider how it turns out. It is simply because your weapons were a bluff that your station still exists: and because it exists, that we still have a foothold on the moon. That is important.'

Troon looked up.

'You think so, too, General? Not very many people do.'

'There are not, at any time, many people who have — what do you call it in Engish? — Divine discontent? Vision? Most men like to be settled among their familiar things, with a notice on the door: "Do Not Disturb." They would still have that notice hanging outside their caves if it were not for the few discontented men. Therefore it is *important* that we are still here, *important* that we do not lose our gains. You understand?'

Troon nodded. He smiled faintly.

'I understand, General. I understand very well. Why did I fight for a Moon Station? Why did I come here, and stay here? To hold on to it so that one day I could say to a younger man: "Here it is. We've got you this far. Now go ahead. The stars are before you ..." Yes, I understand. But what I have had to wonder lately is whether the time will ever come for me to say it. . . .'

General Budorieff nodded. He looked out, long and speculatively, at the pearl-blue Earth.

'Will there be any rocket-ships left? Will there be anyone left to bring them?' he murmured.

Troon looked in the same direction. With the pale earth-light shining in his face he felt a sudden conviction.

'They'll come,' he said. 'Some of them will hear the thin gnat-voices crying. ... They'll have to come. ... And, one day, they'll go on. . . .'

THREE

MARS

A.D. 2094

THE calendar-clock tells me that, at home, it is breakfast-time on the 24th of June. There's no reason, as far as I can see, why that should not be so: if it is, I must have been on Mars for exactly ten weeks. Quite a time; and I wonder how many more weeks to follow . . . ?

One day, other people will come here and find, at least, the ship. I ought to have tried to keep a regular log, but it did not seem worth while – and, anyway, it wouldn't have been regular for long. I have been – well, I have not been quite myself. . . . But now that I have faced facts I am calmer, almost resigned; and I find myself feeling that it would be more creditable not to leave simply a mystery. Someone is sure to come one day; better not to leave him to unravel it by inference alone, and perhaps wrongly. There are some things I want to say, and some I ought to say – besides, it will give me something to occupy my mind. That is rather important to me; I don't want to lose my hold on my mind again if I can help it. Funny, it is the early things that stick: there used, I remember, to be an old drawing-room song to impress the ladies: 'Let me like a soldier fall!' . . . Hammy, of course, and yet . . .

But no need to hurry. There is, I think, still some time to go. . . . I have come out on the other side of something, and now I find in the thought of death a calmness; it is so much less frightening than the thought of life in this place. . . . My regrets have turned outwards – the chief of them is for the distress my Isabella must now be feeling, and for

Mars

the anxieties I must leave her to face alone as George and Anna grow up. . . .

I do not know who is going to read what I am writing. One supposes that it will be some member of an expedition that knows all about us, up to the time of our landing. We gave the bearings of our landing-place on the radio, so there should be no great difficulty in finding the ship where she now lies. But one cannot be sure. Possibly the message was not received: there may be reasons why a long time will pass before she is found. It could even be that she will be discovered accidentally by someone who never heard of us. . . . So, after all, an account may serve better than a log. . . .

I introduce myself: Trunho. Capitão Geoffrey Montgomery Trunho, of the Space Division of the Skyforce of Brazil, lately of Avenida Oito de Maio 138, Pretario, Minas Gerais, Brazil, America do Sul. Citizen of the Estados Unidos do Brasil, aged twenty-eight years. Navigator, and sole-surviving crew-member, of the E.U.B. Spacevessel, *Figurão*.

I am Brasileiro by birth. My grandfather, and my father, were formerly British subjects, and became Brazilian by naturalization in the year 2056, at which time they changed the name from Troon to Trunho, for phonetic convenience.

Our family has a space tradition. My great-great-grandfather was the famous Ticker Troon – the one who rode the rocket, at the building of the first space-station. My great-grandfather was Commander of the British Moon Station at the time of the Great Northern War, and it is likely that my grandfather would have followed him there later, but for the war. It so happened, however, that the war broke out during my grandfather's term of ground-work at the British Space-House – or, to be more accurate, at one of the Space-House's secret and deep-dug operational centres; and it happened, further, that the actual outbreak of hostilities occurred when he was off-base. He was, in fact, on leave in Jamaica, where he had taken his wife (my grandmother) and my father, then aged six, on a visit to his mother's recently bought house.

Many books have been written since the event, showing that that war was inevitable, and that the high councils knew it to be inevitable; but my grandfather always denied that. He maintained that on the highest levels, no less than in the public mind, it had come to be thought of as the-war-that-would-never-happen.

Our leaders may have been foolish; they may, in a long state of deadlock, have been too easily lulled: but they were not criminal lunatics, and they knew what a war must mean. There were, of course, incidents that caused periodical waves of panic, but however troublesome they may have been to trade and to the stock-markets, they were not taken very seriously on the higher political levels, and from a Service point of view were even felt not to be a bad thing. Had the never-happen attitude been quite unperturbed there would, without doubt, have been cuts in Service allocations, technical progress would have suffered in consequence, and too much of a falling-behind could conceivably mean that the Other Fellows would have gained enough ascendancy and superiority in armament to make them think a quick war worth risking.

In the opinion of his own Department, my grandfather asserted, an actual outbreak seemed no more likely than it had seemed two years, or five years, or ten years before. Their work was going on as usual, organizing, reorganizing, and superseding in the light of new discoveries; playing a kind of chess in which one's pieces were lost, not to the opponent, but to obsolescence. There never has been, according to him, any conclusive proof that the war was not touched off by some megalomaniac, or even by accident.

Mars

It had long been axiomatic on both sides that, should missiles arrive, the form was to get one's own missiles into the air as soon as possible, and hit the enemy's potential as fast and as hard as one could – and, in 2044, there was little that could not be considered a part of his potential, from his factories to the morale of his people and the health of his crops.

So, one night, my grandfather went to sleep in a world where peace was no more restive than it had been for years; and in the morning he awoke in one that had been at war for four hours, with casualties already high in the millions.

All over North America, all over Europe, all over the Russian Empire there were flashes that paled the sun, heatwaves that seared and set on fire whole countrysides. Monstrous plumes were writhing up into the sky, shedding ashes, dust, and death.

My grandfather was immediately obsessed by his duty – his obligation to get back somehow to his post, which was that section of the British Service located in northern Canada. For two days he spent nearly all his time in Kingston, badgering the authorities and anyone else he could find.

There were plenty of aircraft there, plenty of all kinds, large airlines, crowded freighters, small owner-flown machines, but they were all coming from the north; most of them pausing only to refuel, and then fleeing on, like migrating birds, to the south. Nothing took off for the north.

Communications were chaotic. No one could tell what fields were still available, still less how long they would remain so. Pilots resolutely refused to take the risk, even for large sums, and the airport authorities backed them up by refusing to sanction any northward flights with an impregnability against which my grandfather, and numbers of anxious United States citizens, battered in vain.

The Outward Urge

On the evening of the second day, however, he succeeded in buying someone out of a seat on a south-bound aircraft, and set off with the intention of making a circuit via Port Natal, in Brazil, Dakar, and Lisbon, and so to England where he hoped to be able to find a Service machine to get him to Canada. In point of fact, he arrived at Freetown, Sierra Leone, about eight days later, and got no further. News there was still scarce and contradictory, but there was enough of it to convince not merely pilots, but everyone else, that even if an aircraft should safely get through, a landing almost anywhere in Europe would mean delayed, if not immediate, suicide.

It took him two months to get home again to Jamaica, by which time, of course, the Northern War was almost history.

It was, however, such recent history that the noncombatants were still numbed by the shock. The near-paralysis of fright which had held everyone outside the war-zone for a month was relaxed, but people had still not fully got over their astonishment at finding themselves and their homes surviving undamaged. Still persisting, too, was that heightened awareness which made each new, untroubled day seem a gracious gift, rather than a right. There was a dazed pause, a sense of coming-to again before the worries of life swept back.

And all too soon the worries were plentiful – not only over radiation, active dusts, contaminated water, diseases threatening both flora and fauna, and such immediate matters; but also over the whole problem of re-orientation in a world where most of a hemisphere had become a malignant, unapproachable desert...

Jamaica, it was clear, was not going to have much to offer except exports for which there was virtually no market. It could sustain itself; one might be able to go on living

Mars

there, with much diminished standards, but it was certainly no place to build a new life.

My grandmother was in favour of a move to South Africa where her father was chairman of the board of a small aircraft company. She argued that my grandfather's knowledge and experience would make him a useful addition to the board, and that with most of the great aircraft factories of the world now destroyed, a tremendous growth of the company was inevitable.

My grandfather was unenthusiastic, but he did go as far as to pay a visit there to talk the matter over with his father-in-law. He returned unconverted, however. He was not, he said, at all taken with the place; there was something about it that made him uneasy. My grandmother, though disappointed, refrained from pressing the matter – which turned out to be fortunate, for a little over a year later her father, and all her relatives there, were among the millions who died in the great African Rising.

But before that took place my grandfather had made his own decision.

'China,' he said, 'is not out, but she has been very badly mauled and reduced – it will take her a long time to recover. Japan has suffered out of proportion to the material damage there because of the concentration of her population. India is weakened, as usual, by her internal troubles. Africa has been kept backward. Australia is the centre of the surviving British, and may one day become an important nation – but it will take time. South America, however, is intact, and looks to me to be the natural focus of world power in the immediate future; and that means either Brazil or the Argentine. I should be very much surprised indeed if it were to turn out to be Argentina. So we shall go to Brazil.'

To Brazil, then, he went, offering his technical knowledge.

The Outward Urge

Almost immediately he was put in charge of the then rudimentary Space Division of the Brazilian Skyforce to organize the annexation of the battered Satellites, to dispatch provision-missiles to the British Moon Station, and then to direct its relief, the rescue of its company – including his father – and its annexation, together with that of the entire Lunar Territory, to the Estados Unidos do Brasil.

The cost of this enterprise, particularly at such a time, was considerable, but it proved to be well justified. Prestige has varied sources. In spite of the fact that the Moon Stations and the Satellites had exerted an infinitesimal, and almost self-cancelling, effect upon the Northern War, the knowledge that they were now entirely in Brazilian hands – and perhaps the thought that whenever the moon rose one was being overlooked from Brazilian territory – undoubtedly made a useful contribution to the ascendancy of the Brasileiros at a time when the disordered remnant of the world was searching for a new centre of gravity.

Once he had the space project well in hand, my grandfather, though not yet a Brazilian citizen, was given the leadership of a mission to British Guiana, where he pointed out the advantages that an amputated colony would derive from integration, on terms of full equality of citizenship, with a powerful neighbour. The ex-colony, already uneasily conscious of pressure on its western border from Venezuela, accepted the offer. A few months later, Surinam and French Guiana followed its example; and the Caribbean Federation signed a treaty of friendship with Brazil. In Venezuela, the government, bereft of North American support and markets, fell to a short, sharp revolution whose leaders also elected for integration with Brazil. Columbia, Ecuador, and Peru hastened to sign treaties of support and friendship. Chile concluded a defensive alliance with Argentina. Bolivia,

Paraguay, and Uruguay were drawn together into nervous neutrality, and declarations of goodwill towards both their powerful neighbours.

My grandfather took out his naturalization papers, and became a loyal and valued citizen of the Republic.

My father graduated from the University of São Paulo in 2062 with a Master's degree in Extra-Terrestrial Engineering, and then spent several years at the government testing-station in the Rio Branco.

It had long been my grandfather's contention that the development of space craft was not simply a matter of prestige, as some thought, and certainly not the expensive frivolity that others proclaimed it, but a wise precaution that would some day prove its worth. For one thing, he argued, if Brazil were to neglect space, someone else would take it over. For another, there would arise, sooner or later, the need for an economic space-freighter. The whole foundation of modern technology rested upon metals; and with the rich metalliferous areas of Canada, Siberia, and Alaska now unworkable; with Africa absorbing all she could mine, India in the market for all she could buy, and South America consuming at an increasing rate, the shortages already apparent in the rarer metals would become more extensive and more acute. The cost, when it should become necessary to seek them in sources outside the Earth, was bound to be great: at present it would be prohibitive, but he did not believe it need remain prohibitive. If practical freighters were developed it could mean that one day Brazil might have a monopoly of at least the rarer metals and metalliferous earths.

How much faith my father had in the argument behind the policy, I do not know. I think it possible that he did not know, either, but used it simply for the problems it raised; and out of all these his hardiest and most favourite concerned what he called 'the crate' — his name for an economical, unmanned freighter — and the space-assembled cruiser. Numbers of 'crates' of various types exist on his drawing-boards, but the cruisers — craft radically different in conception from those that must resist the stresses of take-off against the pull of gravity — still remain somewhat fluid in conception.

I myself, though I inherit my family's almost pathological interest in matters beyond the ionosphere, do not share my father's ability to sublimate it in theory and design, wherefore, after taking my degree at São Paulo, I attended the Skyforce Academy, and was duly commissioned in the Space Division.

A family connexion has its uses. I should not, I am sure, have received preference over better qualified men, but when the original list of twenty volunteers for the appointment of navigator aboard the *Figurão* had been whittled down to four, all equally qualified, I suspect that the name Trunho — and Troon before it — had some influence on the decision.

Raul Capaneiro, our Commander, very likely owed his selection to not unsimilar circumstances, for his father was a Marshal in the Skyforce. But it was not so with Camilo Botoes — he was with us simply because he was unique. His intention of visiting another planet seems to have been formed about the time he was in his cradle, and, not a great deal later it would appear, he had conceived the idea that some unusual qualification would give him an advantage over the one-line man. He set out to acquire it, with the result that when the call for volunteers came, the Skyforce discovered with some surprise that it had among its personnel a capable electronics officer who was also a geologist, and not merely a dabbler, but one whose published papers made it impossible to ignore his competence to produce a preliminary study in areology.

My own appointment to the crew troubled my mother, and distressed my poor Isabella, but its effect on my father was dichotomous. The *Figurão*, the Big Shot, was the product of his department, and largely of his own ideas. Its success would give him a place in history as the designer of the first interplanetary link; if I were to go with it, his connexion would be still more personal, making the venture something of a family affair. On the other hand, I am his only son; and he was sharply conscious that the very best of his skill, care, and knowledge must still leave the ship at the mercy of numerous unguessed hazards. The thought that he would be exposing me to risks he had been unable to forsee, and could not guard against, was in painful conflict with his awareness that any objections he might make to my going would be construed as lack of confidence in his own work. Thus, I put him in a rendingly difficult situation; and now I wish, almost more than anything else, that I had the means to tell him that it is not through any shortcoming of his that I shall not be going home to Earth ...

The launch took place on the 9th of December, a Wednesday. The preliminary jump was quite uneventful, and we followed the usual supply-rocket practice in our intersection with the Satellite orbit, and in taking up station close to the Satellite itself.

I felt sentimentally glad that the station was Esatrellita Primeira; it made the expedition even more of a family affair, for it was the first space-station, the one that my great-great-grandfather had helped to build – though I suppose that most parts of it must have been replaced on account of war and other damage since those days.

We crossed over to Primeira, and put in more than a

week of Earth-days there while the *Figurão*'s atmosphere-protection envelope was removed, and she was refuelled and fully provisioned. The three of us carried out tests in our various departments, and made a few necessary minor adjustments. Then we waited, almost wishing there had been more readjustments to keep us occupied, until Primeira, the Moon, and Mars were in the relative positions calculated for our take-off. At last, however, on Tuesday, the 22nd of December, at 0335 R.M.T., we made blast and launched ourselves on the main journey.

I shall not deal here with the journey itself. All technical information concerning it has been entered by Raul in the official log, which I shall enclose, with this supplementary account, in a metal box.

What I have written so far has two purposes. One is, as I have said, to cover the possibility that it may not be found for a very long time; the other is to provide factual material by which any more imminent finder may check my mental condition. I have read carefully through it myself, and to me it appears to offer sufficient evidence that I am sane and coherent, and I trust that that will be the opinion of others who may read it, and that they may therefore consider what follows to be equally valid.

The final entry in the log will be seen to record that we were approaching Mars on a spiral. The last message we sent before landing will be found on the file: 'About to attempt landing area Isidis–Syrtis Major. Intended location: Long., 275: Lat., 48.'

When Camilo had dispatched that message, he swung the transmitter across on its bracket to lock it safely against the wall, and then lay back on his couch. Raul and I were already in position on ours. My work was finished, and I had nothing to do but wait. Raul had the extension control panel clamped across his couch in a position where he would still be able to operate it against a pressure of several gravities, if necessary. Everything had gone according to expectations except that our outer surface temperature was somewhat higher than had been calculated – suggesting that the atmosphere is a trifle denser than has been assumed – but the error was small, and of little practical significance.

Raul set about adjusting the angle of the ship, tilting her to preserve the inclination in relation to the braking thrust as we slowed. Our couches turned on their gimbals as the speed decreased and the braking thrust of the main tubes gradually became our vertical support. Finally, when the speed was virtually zero, and we were standing balanced on our discharge, his job, too, was over. He switched in the landing-control, and lay back, watching the progress of our descent, on the dials.

Beneath us, there now splayed downwards eight narrow radar beams matched for proximity, and each controlling a small lateral firing-tube. The least degree of tilt was registered by one or more of the beams, and corrected by a short blast which restored the ship to balance on the point of the main drive. Another beam directed vertically downwards controlled the force of the main drive itself, relating it to the distance of the surface below, and thus regulating the speed of descent.

The arrangement lowered us, smoothly, and there was only the slightest of lurches as our supporting tripod set down. Then the drive cut out, vibration ceased, and an almost uncanny peace set in.

No one spoke. The completeness of the silence began to be broken by the ticking and clicking of metal cooling off. Presently Raul sat up, and loosed his safety straps.

'Well, we're there. Your old man did a good job,' he said to me.

The Outward Urge

He got off his couch carefully, cautious of the unfamiliar feeling of gravity, and made for the nearest port. I did the same, and started to unscrew its cover. Camilo swung the radio over on its bracket, and transmitted: '*Figurão* landed safely Mars 0343 R.M.T. 18.4.94. Location believed as stated. Will observe and verify.' Then he, too, reached for the nearest port-cover.

The view, when I had my port uncovered, was much what I had expected; an expanse of hummocky, rust-red desert sand reaching away to the horizon. Anywhere else, it would have been the least exciting of all possible views. But it was not anywhere else: it was Mars, seen as no one had ever seen it before ... We did not cheer, we did not slap one another on the back. ... We just went on staring at it. ...

At last Raul said, rather flatly:

'There it is, then. Miles and miles of nothing; and all of it ours.'

He turned away, and went over to a row of dials.

'Atmosphere about fifteen per cent denser than predicted; that accounts for the overheating,' he said. 'We'll have to wait for the hull to cool down a bit before we can go out. Oxygen content very low indeed – by the look of things, most of it has been tied up in oxidizing these deserts.' He went over to a locker, and started pulling out space-suits and gear. He did it clumsily; after weeks of weightlessness it is difficult to remember that things will drop if you let go of them.

'Funny that error about atmosphere density,' said Camilo.

'Not so very,' Raul replied. 'Just that someone's crackpot theory about air leaking away into space got written into the assumptions, I reckon. Why the devil should it leak away unless there is a large body around to attract it? Might as well suggest that our own atmosphere is leaking to the moon, and then back again. Beats me how these loony

Mars

propositions get a foot in, but I expect we'll find plenty more of them.'

'Were they wrong about gravity, too?' I asked. 'I seem to feel a lot heavier than I expected.'

'No. That's as calculated. Just a matter of getting used to weight itself,' he said.

I crossed the floor, and looked through the port that he had uncovered. The view was almost the same as through mine – though not quite, for in that direction the meeting of sand and sky was marked by a thin dark line. I wondered what it was. At that distance I could see no detail – nor, indeed, judge how far away the horizon was. I turned back, intending to find the eyepiece that would adapt the telescope, but at that moment the floor shifted under my feet. . . .

The whole room canted over suddenly, sliding me across the floor. The heavy port cover swung over. It just missed me, but it caught Raul, and sent him slamming against the main control-board. The room tilted more. I was flung back on the couch I had just left, and I clung to it. Camilo came sliding past, trying to grab at the couch supports to stop himself.

There were several thuds, a clatter, and finally a kind of crunching crash which set me bouncing on the couch springs.

When I looked round I found that what had, for the brief period since our landing, been the floor, had become a vertical wall. Obviously the *Figurão* had toppled over, and now lay on its side. Camilo was huddled in the angle made by the erstwhile floor and the curved wall, all mixed up with the space-suits and their accessories. Raul was spreadeagled over the control-board, and I could see blood trickling across it.

I dropped off the couch, and approached Raul. I started

to lift his head, but it did not come easily. Then I found out why. It had crashed down on one of the control levers, and the handle had gone in at the temple. There was nothing to be done for him. I scrambled across, and looked at Camilo. He was unconscious, but there was no visible damage. His pulse was strong enough, and I set about trying to bring him round. Several minutes went by before his eyes opened, then they looked at me, screwed up, with lids fluttering, and closed again. I found some brandy. Presently he sighed, and his eyes opened again. They looked at me, wandered about the control room, and came back to me again.

'Mars,' he said. 'Mars, the bloody planet. Is this Mars?'

There was a silly look about him that made my spirits sink.

'Yes, this is Mars,' I told him.

I lifted him on to one of the couches, and made him comfortable there. His eyes closed, and he went off again.

I looked round. The only part of the equipment, other than the space-suits, that had been loose was the radio-transmitter. Camilo, after using it had pushed it aside, leaving it free to swing on its bracket; it had done just that, and been stove-in when it met one of the couches turning in its gimbals. It looked suitable for writing-off.

I couldn't just sit there, doing nothing but look at the other two, so I disentangled one suit, and coupled it up with its air-supply and batteries, and tested it. It worked perfectly. The thermometer giving the outside hull reading was down quite a bit from what it had been, and I decided to go outside to find the trouble.

Fortunately, as the ship lay, the airlock was at the side, the right side as one faced forward; had it been underneath, it would have been extremely difficult, if not impossible, to get out at all. Even as we lay, it was awkward enough,

Mars

for the lock had been built to accommodate two men standing, and now one had to sit doubled up inside it. It worked, however – though when the outer door opened, the telescopic ladder could not be made to project at a suitable angle. I had to get out by jumping down six feet or so, and my first contact with the surface of Mars was undignified.

To stand there at last was, in the event, depressing. Not just because the only view was arid miles of red sand, but even more because I was alone.

It was the moment we had thought and talked of for so long, worked so hard for, risked so much for – and this was all. Anticlimax there would surely have been, but it would have been less dreary with someone to share it, with a little ceremony to mark the occasion. Instead, I just stood there, alone. Under the small, weak sun in the purplish sky I was dwindled to a tiny living mote with the barren wilderness pressing all about me....

Not that it was different from my expectations – in fact, it looked only too like them – and yet I knew now that in all my imaginings I had never remotely touched its real quality. I had thought of it as empty and neutral; never suspected its implicit hostility....

Yet there was nothing there, nothing to be afraid of – except the worst thing of all: fear itself. The fear that has no cause, shape, or centre; that same amorphous fear that used to come creeping out of the dark, massing to invade the safety of one's childish bed....

I could feel the old panic, forgotten for so many years, rising up again. I was back in my infant self; all that I had learnt in the years between seemed to vanish; once more, I was the defenceless, beset by the incomprehensible. I wanted to run back to the ship, as to my mother, for safety. I all but did that....

The Outward Urge

Yet not quite.... A vestige of my rational mind held me there. It kept on telling me that if I gave in to panic now, it would be far worse the next time, and the time after.... And gradually, while I stood, the vestige gathered the strength to push the panic back. Soon I could feel it winning, like warm blood flowing in. Then I felt better. I was able to force some objectivity.

I looked carefully round. From this low viewpoint there was no trace anywhere of the dark line that I had seen through the port when the *Figurão* was vertical. All the way round, red sand met purple sky in an endless, even line. There was nothing, nothing at all, on the face of the desert but the ship and myself under the centre of a vast, upturned bowl.

Then I made myself pay attention to the ship. It was easy to see what had happened. Below the light dust of the surface, the sand had formed a crust. Our weight had caused the pediment plate on one of the tripod legs to break through the crust, and we had toppled over. I wondered for a moment if Raul would be able to contrive some way of getting us vertical again – and then suddenly recollected why he would not....

I went back into the ship, and looked for something to dig with. Camilo had not moved, and appeared to have fallen into a natural sleep. Luckily, someone had thought of equipping the ship with a sort of entrenching tool. It was small, but it would have to do. Getting Raul outside was unpleasant, and far from easy, but I managed it, and laid him on the sand while I dug. That was not easy work, either, in a space-suit, and I thought it might take me several shifts. But at about twelve inches down I suddenly broke through, and found myself looking into a black hole. Considering the misadventure to the ship, it seemed possible that the place was honeycombed with such cavities. I enlarged the

Mars

hole a little until I was able to slide poor Raul into it. Then I blocked the opening with a slab of caked sand, covered it as best I could, and went back to the ship again.

I came out of the airlock to find that Camilo was now awake – not only awake, but sitting up on his couch, regarding me with nervous intensity.

'I don't like Martians,' he said.

I looked at him more carefully. His expression was serious, and not at all friendly.

'I don't suppose I would, either,' I admitted, keeping my tone matter-of-fact.

His expression became puzzled, then wary. He shook his head.

'Very cunning lot, you Martians,' he remarked.

After we had had a meal he seemed a little better, though from time to time I caught him watching me carefully out of the corner of his eye. Indeed, he was paying so much attention to me that it was some time before it occurred to him that there should be three of us.

'Where's Raul?' he asked.

I explained what had happened to Raul, showed him the switch lever that had done the fatal damage, and pointed out through the port the place where Raul now lay. He listened closely, and nodded several times, though not always where a nod seemed appropriate. It was difficult to know whether he was not quite grasping the situation, or whether he was making reservations of his own. He did not show distress about Raul, only a quiet thoughtfulness, and after he had sat in silent rumination on the matter for a quarter of an hour, it began to get on my nerves.

To break it up, I showed him the radio transmitter.

'It's taken a pretty nasty bash,' I said, somewhat unnecessarily. 'Do you think you can get it going again?'

The Outward Urge

Camilo looked it over for some minutes.

'It certainly has,' he agreed.

'Yes,' I said impatiently, 'but the point is, can you fix it?'

He turned his head, and looked at me steadily.

'You want to get into touch with Earth,' he announced.

'Of course we do. They'll be expecting reports from us right now. They know our time of landing, but that's all, so far. We've got to put in an immediate report about Raul, and about the state of the ship. Tell them the mess we're in. . . .

He considered that in an unhurried way, and then shook his head, doubtfully.

'I don't know,' he said. 'You're so cunning, you Martians.'

'Oh, for heaven's sake – !' I began, but then made a quick decision that it might be unwise to antagonize him. Rather than drive him into obstinacy, I tried to put across a calmly persuasive line.

He listened patiently, with a slight frown, as one taking into consideration every possible angle. At the end, still without committing himself on whether he thought he could make the radio work or not, he said that it was an important matter that required thinking over. I could only hold my temper for fear of setting up a worse conflict in his mind.

He retreated to his couch and lay on it, presumably to do his important thinking. I stood looking out of the port a while, and then, realizing that the day would soon be coming to an end, got out the colour camera and busied myself with making the first records ever of the stages of a Martian sunset.

This was not a spectacular affair. The small sun grew somewhat redder as it dropped towards the horizon. As it disappeared from sight, the sky turned immediately from purple to black – all except a wispy stretch of cloud, quite surprising to me, which still caught the rays, glowing pinkly for a minute or two, and then vanished. Looking through another port I could see a small bright disc just above the rim, and climbing almost visibly up the spangled blackness. I took it to be Phobos, and turned the telescope on to it. It does not appear to be of any great interest; not unlike our own moon, but less mountainous, and much less cratered.

All the time I was uneasily conscious of Camilo. Whenever I took a look in his direction I found his head turned my way, and his eyes watching me in a speculative fashion that was difficult to disregard. I did my best, however, and busied myself with fixing the camera to the telescope. The speed of the satellite rendered it none too easy to keep it centred in the field of view, but I made a number of exposures. Camilo had fallen asleep again by the time I had finished, and I was tired enough to be glad to get on my own couch.

Once I had dropped off I slept heavily. When I woke, there was daylight outside the ports, and Camilo standing beside one of them looking out. He must have heard me move for he said, without turning:

'I don't like Mars.'

'Nor do I,' I agreed. 'But then, I never expected to.'

'Funny thing,' he said. 'I got it into my head last night that you were a Martian. Sorry.'

'You had a nasty knock,' I told him. 'Must have shaken you up quite a bit. How are you feeling now?'

'Oh, all right – bit of a muzzy headache. It'll pass. Damn silly of me thinking you were a Martian. You're not a bit like one, really.'

I was in the middle of a yawn, and failed to finish it properly.

The Outward Urge

'What,' I inquired, with some caution, 'what *are* Martians like?'

'That's the trouble,' he said, still looking out of the port. 'It's so hard to see them properly. They're so quick. When you're looking at one place, you see a flicker of them moving in another, just out of the corner of your eye, and by the time you look there they're somewhere else.'

'Oh,' I said. 'But, you know, I never noticed any when I was outside yesterday.'

'But you weren't looking for them,' Camilo pointed out, and truly.

I swung my feet off the couch.

'What about some breakfast,' I suggested.

He agreed, but remained by the window while I set about getting things ready – an awkward job with a curved wall for a floor, and everything at right angles from its intended position. Now and then he would glance quickly from one side of the view to the other, often with a little sound of exasperation as though he had just missed something again. It was irritating, but on the whole a slight improvement on being taken for a Martian myself.

'Come and eat,' I told him when I had the food ready. 'They'll keep.'

He left the port with some reluctance, but started in on the food with a good appetite.

'Do you think you'll be able to fix the radio?' I inquired presently.

'Maybe,' he said, 'but is it wise?'

'Why the devil shouldn't it be?' I demanded, with some restraint.

'Well,' he explained, 'they might intercept our messages. And if they learn what a mess we're in it could very likely encourage them to attack.'

'We'll have to take a chance on that. The important thing

for us is to get into touch with home, and see what they suggest. It seems to me possible, just possible, that we may be able to get the ship back to the vertical somehow – with the gravitation as low as it is. I can plot the course and time of take-off, and look after that side, but can we manage her without Raul? He was the one with experience and special training. I have a *general* idea of the controls, and I suppose you have, but it is only general. This ship isn't build to stand up to the strains of ordinary take-offs – that's why she had to have a special casing to get her from Earth to Primeira. She must have a specially calculated programme of safe velocities for take-off from here – and that will have to be amended on account of the atmosphere being denser than was reckoned. We don't want to burn her up, or melt her tubes. As things are, I don't begin to know about her acceleration schedule, her safety-factors. Damn it, I don't even know off-hand the escape velocity of Mars.'

'It should take you all of two minutes to work that out,' Camilo interrupted.

'I dare say, but there are a hell of a lot of things we can't work out without the data. Some of it we'll be able to get from Raul's technical papers no doubt, but there are bound to be all kinds of questions arising that we shall need advice about.'

'M'm,' said Camilo, doubtfully. His eyes strayed towards one of the ports for a moment, and then came back to me, looking suspicious again. 'You didn't talk to them while you were out there?' he asked.

'Oh hell,' I said impatiently, and unwisely. 'Look, there's nothing out there – nothing but sand. Come out with me, and see for yourself.'

He shook his head slowly, and gave me the smile of a man who knows a trick worth two of that.

I was at a loss to know what line to take next. After I had

The Outward Urge

thought about it a bit, it seemed to me that we were not going to get far while he was worried by these Martian phantoms, and the sooner they could be laid, the better.

Perhaps I was wrong there. Perhaps I ought simply to have waited, hoping that the effect of the concussion would wear off. After all, except for the anxiety that must be going on at the other end of our radio link, there was no pressing hurry. The sun-charger would keep our batteries up, even at this distance from the sun; water is on an almost closed circuit, with very little loss, air regeneration too; there was victualling enough to last two of us for eighteen months. I *could* have waited. But it is one thing to consider a situation retrospectively, and quite another to be at close quarters with a single companion who is slightly off his head, and wondering whether time is likely to make him better or worse. . . .

However, as the radio seemed to be in some way entangled in his mind with the intentions of his cunning Martians, I decided to lay aside that subject of the moment, and tried tackling him on his other speciality. I pulled out a lump of the caked sand that I had brought inside, and handed it to him.

'What do you reckon that is?' I asked.

He gave it the briefest of glances.

'Haematite – Fe_2O_3,' he said, looking at me as if I had asked a pretty stupid question. 'Mars,' he said, patiently, 'is practically all oxides of one kind or another. This'll be the commonest.'

'I've been thinking,' I said. 'One of our main objects, after getting here at all, is to bring in a preliminary report on the geology of Mars.'

'Areology,' he corrected me. 'You can't possibly talk about the geology of Mars. Doesn't make sense.'

'All right, areology,' I agreed, finding his lucidity encouraging and irritating at the same time. 'Well, we can at least make a start on that. There is a dark line on the horizon, over that way, that wants looking into – might be vegetation of some kind. If we get the platform out, we could have a look at it, and at the topography in general, too.'

I made the suggestion with a casual air, and awaited his answer with some anxiety, for I felt that if I could use his geological – or areological – interests to lure him outside, even a brief expedition might serve to dispel this notion of lurking Martians, and once that had been achieved, he would be willing to get on with the repair of the radio.

He did not reply immediately, and I restrained myself from looking up for fear of seeming anxious enough to rouse his suspicions. At last, when I had started to consider the next step, he said:

'They wouldn't be able to reach us once the platform lifted, would they?'

'Of course not – if they are there at all. I've not seen one yet,' I said, trying not to give any encouraging support to his fancies.

'I *nearly* saw one half a minute ago. But they're always just too damned quick, blast them,' he complained.

'There'd be no hiding from overhead observation in this desert,' I pointed out. 'If they are there, we'll be able to spot them easily from the platform.'

'*If* – ' he began indignantly, and then stopped, apparently struck by an idea. After a pause he went on in a quite different tone:

'All right. Yes, that's a good idea. Let's locate the platform, and start getting it out.'

His change of front was sudden enough to make me look at him in astonishment. His expression now was enthusiastic, and he gave an encouraging nod. Apparently I had

The Outward Urge

chosen the right line, though I hoped he would not back off the idea with the same unexpectedness that he had veered on to it. At the moment, however, he was certainly all for it, and pulled a file of papers out of a locker.

'The loading plan ought to be here,' he said. 'I'm pretty sure the platform was stowed in Number Two hold-section....'

It was soon pretty clear that Camilo's 'let's' was a manner of speaking. What he meant was that I should get the platform out. I made one attempt at persuading him to put on a space-suit, and give me a hand, but he was so clearly averse to that that I gave up rather than risk having him turn against the whole idea. Once I had it assembled, and he could step straight on to it, I could lift it at once, and *show* him that nothing could be lurking in that desert. So presently I went out alone, and opened up Number Two hold-section to get the platform out.

There had been something of a tussle over the provision of a jet-platform for us. The type that had proved itself on the moon over fifty years ago would not do: there, an object has only one-sixth of its earth-weight; on Mars, it weighs double its moon-weight, and therefore any carrier must be heavier and more powerful. A wheeled vehicle would have been much lighter, but we were opposed to that for use on an unknown terrain. A platform could skim safely above any kind of surface, and my father had supported us. In the end, he had designed a suitable platform in three sections which were dispatched to Primeira to be stowed aboard the *Figurão* when she called there. Thus, for the main lift we had been spared the weight of the biggest single piece of equipment that we carried, and could simply jettison it on Mars when we took off for the return.

I found the three main sections, even at their Martian

weight, quite as much as I wanted to handle, encumbered by my space-suit. Once I had them laid out side by side on the sand, however, the bolting together was comparatively easy.

Camilo had switched on the helmet-radio belonging to one of the other space-suits. From time to time he inquired:

'Have you seen any of them yet?'

Each time I assured him that I had not but, somehow, whether he answered or remained silent, he managed to convey scepticism.

When the main floor was assembled, I went ahead with fixing the control-pillar. Thoroughly absorbed in the job, I lost all sense of my surroundings, remembering the empty stillness only when Camilo spoke. But when, after some two and a half hours, I had the assembly complete and needing only a final check before the mounting of the fuel containers, my attention slackened and, with that, the bleakness and loneliness all about seemed to press closer and crowd me.

I decided I had put in a long enough spell outside for one day, and would be wiser to get back to the familiarity of the ship and the comfort of a meal before the willies could encroach enough to trouble me badly. As I came through the airlock I found Camilo seated on the pull-out stool in front of my charting-board. He turned round and watched me attentively; when I took off the helmet he seemed to relax, and looked somewhat relieved. I glanced at the radio-transmitter, hoping that he might have started to tackle that, but it was clear that it had not been touched.

He asked how things were going, and nodded when I told him.

'We'll need the two-man dome, and gear for it, and of course the fuel containers – might as well unload the lot of them while you're at it; just as well to have them stacked

The Outward Urge

handy; no point in leaving them in the ship. And some cases of food, and bottles of water, and –'

'Steady on,' I protested. 'We shan't be going on a week's expedition right away. All I expect to do tomorrow is to try the thing out, and perhaps have a short flip over to see what that dark line is. We can take the dome and some food against an emergency, but there's no point in loading up useless extra weight.'

'Tomorrow?' he repeated. 'I thought – I mean, there's about five hours of light yet. . . .'

'Possibly,' I admitted, 'but I've just done nearly three hours steady work in a space-suit. If you are so anxious to hurry it on, you try a shift on the job yourself.'

I had scarcely expected him to rise to that, and he didn't. Instead he watched me for a minute or two without speaking, while I collected some food. Then he went back to looking out of the window. He'd stand there, motionless, peering intently for a time, then he would suddenly turn his head quickly from side to side, like a spectator watching an unnaturally fast rally at a tennis match, and draw his breath in quickly. After that, there would be another motionless interlude for a bit. I was already edgy from the spell outside, and it soon began to get on my nerves.

'You won't see anything,' I told him. 'Come over here, and have some food.'

Rather surprisingly, he came without demur.

'I suppose you told them to keep out of sight,' he said. 'Well, they're doing it, but they aren't fooling me.'

'Oh, for God's sake – !' I began, letting my temper slip a bit at last.

'All right – all right,' he said, hurriedly. 'Perhaps *they* told *you* not to let on about them. It doesn't matter, really. Comes to the same thing.'

I gave up trying to follow that, and simply grunted.

Mars

During the rest of the meal, and after it, we maintained a state of tactful truce, but when this had been disturbed some five times by his leaping to a port in an attempt to catch his Martians unaware, I was driven to suggesting a game of chess to keep our attention occupied. It worked pretty well, too. For a time he seemed to forget all about hostile Martians, played a well-considered game, and beat me by a better margin than usual. At the end of it, things felt much more normal until he remarked:

'That's just it, you see. You Martians are cunning, all right, but not quite cunning enough. We can beat you every time, if we put our minds to it.'

The next morning I went outside and finished checking over the platform, then I got a couple of fuel containers out of the hold-section and mounted them. Camilo, watching through the port, repeated on the helmet-radio his suggestion of unloading them all. I appreciated that by lightening the ship there would be an advantage when it came to an attempt to raise her to the vertical, but they were heavy, and I did not see why I should do all the work – that part could wait until Camilo was in a state where he was willing to come out and help. I did add a case of food, a couple of bottles of water – and also the two-man Flandrys Dome, for it isn't much good carrying rations against an emergency unless you also provide somewhere to take off your helmet so that you can eat them. And then there had to be the recompression gear to deflate the dome after use, and a matter of half a dozen small standby airbottles for the suits. Altogether, it took me nearly an hour to stow and make fast that lot, but then, at last, I was ready to make a test.

I stepped aboard, and told Camilo to stand by and observe. I tried the under-jets individually first, and they all responded satisfactorily. Then I put them in concert. The platform throbbed, and a large cloud of red dust blew out from beneath it. It lifted, slightly up by the near right-hand corner. I trimmed and levelled her off about eighteen inches above the ground; then, when she was stabilized, took her up to ten feet. At that height I slanted and slid her a bit in each direction, and she answered well. She felt more solid and steadier than a lunar-type platform; a little less sensitive, too – better that than the other way, I thought. I raised her to a hundred feet or so, with a smooth lift.

From there I had a real view. The dark line was revealed as no longer just a line, but as a wide stretch of darker ground reaching away into the distance. To the north and to the south the desert was spread out in utter monotony, but on the eastern horizon there were hills – once mountains, perhaps, but now ground down and rounded off, like very old molars.

I reported to Camilo, but he was not interested in the landscape. He demanded:

'Can you see any of *them*?'

'No,' I told him. 'There aren't any.'

'I don't believe you.'

'Very well. Just put on a space-suit, and come up and see for yourself,' I suggested.

'Oh, no you don't. I wasn't born yesterday. That's how you got Geoff.'

'What the hell are you talking about? I *am* Geoff,' I protested.

'It's no good trying that on me. I know your game, and it's not going to work this time.'

'But look here, Camilo – '

'I know what happened. When poor old Geoff went outside soon after we landed, you were waiting for him. You jumped him, invaded him, turned the real Geoff out, and

Mars

you've been using his body as a disguise. But I spotted you right away. Now you want to get me outside so that another of you can do the same to me. Well, you aren't going to bring that off. Poor old Geoff hadn't been warned, but I have; so it won't work.'

I started to bring the platform down.

'Camilo,' I told him, 'stop talking a lot of bloody nonsense, there's a good fellow. If you don't know me after being cooped up with me all these weeks, you damned well ought to. I never heard such a fantastic, rubbishy –'

'Oh, you put up a very good show,' said Camilo generously. 'Very cunning you are – but it's just because I *do* know Geoff so well that I could spot you.'

I hovered at a foot or so, and let her down gently. She made a nice easy touch, though she blew a cart-load of dust about.

'I've seen through your little idea, too,' he went on. 'You've spotted a chance to get away from this god-forsaken planet. And I don't blame you; anybody in his senses would do his best to get off this ball of sand. So you want to take over this ship, and get to Earth on her. But you aren't going to do it. Not this time, you're not.'

I tried my most authoritative voice.

'Lieutenant Botoes,' I ordered, 'put on a suit, and come out here.'

He laughed.

'Think you've got me, don't you? You toppled the ship over, killed Raul, then you pushed Geoff out of himself and took him over. I'm the only obstacle now, aren't I? But you haven't got me yet. I'll soon show you.'

Then there was a clang that hurt my ears. I guessed he had been holding the helmet to speak into its radio, and had now dropped it. Then I saw the outer door of the lock swing shut. I ran to it, and battered on it, telling him not to be a

The Outward Urge

fool. I had the winding-key to open it from outside, but it would be no good trying that for a minute or more – to attempt it while the automatic mechanism was still securing it would simply have taken me round with the handle.

I went to the port. It was just a little too high for me to see in, so I jumped, in order to get a glimpse of what he was up to. At the same moment the port went blank as the cover closed.

I hurried back to the airlock door, put the key in, and began to wind the locking-bolts back. The tell-tale inside must have shown him what I was up to, for the key suddenly reversed in my hands as the mechanism started again. I swore, and snatched it out.

'Camilo!' I called, hoping my voice would reach him from the dropped helmet. 'Camilo, you've got it all wrong. Don't be a damned fool! Let me in!'

His only reply was, very faintly, a jeering laugh.

'Camilo – ' I was beginning again, when suddenly the ship trembled, and there was a huge spurt of dust and sand, forward. I hadn't a moment's doubt what that meant, and I ran for my life.

Even encumbered with the suit, I covered the ground with great, leaping strides a dozen yards long, and was some eighty yards away in a few seconds, before I misjudged my step and fell.

Still sprawling, I looked back at the *Figurão*. A cloud of dust and sand was spurting from beneath her forepart. Some of the grit was pattering on my helmet. As I watched, the forepart swayed, and then lifted clear of the ground. Most of the loose stuff had been blown away, and I could see the ship better now; well enough to guess what Camilo was trying to do. The three lowermost steering-jets were blasting fiercely as they lifted her nose. I could see the idea, but

I doubted whether he would get enough thrust out of those small jets to push her back to the vertical.

He turned up the power, and she lifted a little more on the two exposed legs of the tripod; no longer nose-down, but tilted a little above the horizontal.

I judged he had the jets on full power. They were holding her up; making a third supporting leg, but they weren't raising her nose any further. I suddenly understood why he had been so anxious to have the platform out of her, and the fuel, and the rest of the stuff, too. Freed of them, she might just have had power enough, but with most of the gear still aboard, she was still inclined only very slightly above the horizontal. The jets kept on roaring and gushing, but still they gave her no more lift. I wondered if it was the leg that had broken through the crust that was keeping her anchored. Clearly she was not going to be able to make it....

Then the main drive fired! Crazy... crazy!

I suppose he thought that, if he could tear the buried leg free, the side-jets would be able to tilt her nose skyward.

She leapt forward, almost horizontal, and with the pediment of the trailing leg dragging a furrow through the sand, like a huge plough-share. She dipped by the head, bounced her belly on the sand, rose again on the supporting side-jets, and he let the main drive have it again.

By God, it was well tried! For a moment I thought he had done it. She lifted until the foot of the trailing leg was barely touching the sand. She was accelerating fast, but at such an angle to me that I could see little more than a cloud of dust with an exhaust flare in the middle of it.

She must, I suppose, have dipped again – and touched. I can't say. All I saw was the silver shape leaping suddenly above the dust cloud, turning over and over in the air, with her drive still flaring. She fell back into the dust, and bounced to appear again; she didn't go so high, and she was spinning differently this time. Then once more she disappeared, and the dust and the sand sprayed up, looking like a shell-burst at sea. . . .

I put down my head, hugged myself to the ground, and waited. . . . She was, I guessed, nearly three miles away by now, but that was unpleasantly close for the kind of explosion I was expecting. I held my breath as I waited . . . and waited. . . .

The explosion did not come.

At last, I looked up, cautiously. Of the *Figurão* herself I could see nothing. There was just a dust-cloud – with a red flare still burning steadily in the middle of it.

I went on waiting. Nothing happened except that the lighter dust was blown away, and the cloud grew smaller. After some more minutes I risked standing up. Scarcely taking my eyes from the spot, I made my way back to the platform. I found it half-buried in sand thrown up by the *Figurão's* blast, but it lifted all right, and the sand slid off as I tilted it and slid it away to a safer distance, to land again.

For over an hour I sat on the platform, watching. Gradually the loose sand and dust had been blown away, and I could see the silver glint of the ship herself, and the steady flame from her tubes.

I realized that somehow, perhaps on the first bounce, the main drive had been reduced to a pretty low power, or the ship would have gone a lot further and fared a lot worse, but I still did not know whether she was going to blow up or not – and, if not, how long the fuel would continue to burn at the present setting.

Perhaps Camilo had been able to check the power at the moment of the first bounce, but he could have had no chance after that. One could not imagine that, even strapped to the couch as he would be, either he himself or the gimbal system could have withstood what the *Figurão* had been through. . . .

And at that thought I was suddenly swept by the terrifying realization that, whether the ship blew up or not, I was now alone. . . .

Almost in the same moment I became aware again of the hostile desert all around. I began to feel the awfulness of utter desolation stalking in on me once more. . . .

I pulled the two-man dome off the platform and set it up. Flimsy though it was, one could find some illusion of protection inside it. The howling of the wilderness was not quite so close to my elbow; the prowling of the agoraphobic monsters was kept a little further off. . . .

The day wore on. The puny red sun declined and disappeared. The constellations shone out, familiar still, for against the panorama of the heavens the leap from Earth to Mars is the tiniest of hops. One day, I am sure, the constellations will look different, when our hops have indeed become great leaps – for me that is an article of faith – but it won't be for a long time yet. . . .

The night closed down. Through the dome's small windows all but the stars was dark – except at one point where, across miles of sand, I could see the glow of the *Figurão*'s main jet, still flaring where she lay.

I broke open a packet of rations, and ate some food. I felt no hunger, but the familiarity of the simple act of eating held some comfort. The food did me good, too. It gave me strength, and I felt better able to resist. Then, suddenly, I became aware of silence. . . .

Looking out of the window again, I saw that the flare of the rocket-tube had vanished. There was nothing but blackness and the stars. All sound had ceased, and left such a silence as was never known on Earth. Nor was it just that, not just the negative absence of sound; the silence was hard, positive, a quality of eternity itself. It rang in one's ears until they sought relief by hearing sounds that did not exist; murmurings, far-off bells, sighs not so far off, tickings, whispers, faint ululations. . . .

A bit of verse that my grandfather used to quote came into my mind:

> . . . for all the night
> I heard their thin gnat-voices cry
> Star to faint star across the sky,

and I seemed to hear them, too: they had no words, they were on the threshold of sound, but they encouraged me. . . .

And, God knows, I needed encouragement, crouched there in my flimsy dome. . . .

The voices cry – but the elemental terrors prowl. We need numbers to sustain us; in numbers we can dispel the terrors; alone, we are weak, mutilated. Taken from our pool of corporate strength we gasp, we wriggle defencelessly while the terrors circle round, slowly closing in. . . .

Perhaps the voices are just sirens – but I think not. I think they are the calls of destiny, leading, not luring, onward and outward. I think we shall, we must, follow them – but not like this! Never again like this! Not, oh God – alone. . . !

The little sun rode over the horizon like a delivering knight. I almost knelt in worship of him as he drove the fingering terrors from my side – not away, but further off, giving me the room, and the courage, to move.

I had meant to eat again, but I could not wait for that. I craved only for the security of the ship. I put my helmet on with shaking hands, packed the dome aboard the platform, lifted to a few feet, and sped across the sand towards the *Figurão* as fast as I could.

Two of the tripod legs were twisted and bent, and the

third torn off, but the hull was surprisingly little damaged I had to clear a lot of sand to get at the airlock as the ship now lay. Much of it I managed to blow away with the platform's jets, but the rest I had to scrape out.

The lock worked perfectly. Inside the ship there was far less damage than I had expected – except to poor Camilo.

I take some pride in having been able to force myself outside again to bury him, as I had buried Raul. I knew that it must be done at once if I were to be able to face it at all so, somehow, I did it. And then hurried back. . . .

It was after that that the gap comes – a long gap, according to the calendar-clock. It looks as if I spent some part of it trying to repair the radio-transmitter; for some reason I seem to have rigged up a light to shine out of each port; the platform is still outside, but not quite as I left it when I first came in. . . . Probably there are other things . . . I don't know . . . I can't remember. . . .

Perhaps someone will come. . . .

I have food enough for nearly three years. . . .

Food enough – but not, I fear, spirit enough. . . .

There is a letter here for my dear Isabella. Give it to her, please. . . .

FOUR

VENUS

A.D. 2144

AFTER George Troon had read the message, he pushed it across to his second-in-command. Arthur Dogget took it, considered it, and then nodded slowly.

'So it's out at last. I'd give a lot to see the Rio papers today. Apoplectic'll be an understatement for 'em,' he said, with some satisfaction. 'Ought to be fun. Two hundred million Brasileiros all steamed up and demanding immediate action. What do you think'll happen?'

Troon shrugged.

'As far as we are concerned, no change. Even a million million wrathful Brasileiros can't affect celestial mathematics. The powers that be have still got to wait for next conjunction before they can come after us. Meanwhile, I suppose the government will throw a few Ministers to the wolves, and assure everybody that retribution is well in hand.'

'They're lucky they've only got six months of it to weather. What surprises me is that they managed to keep it dark so long,' Arthur said. 'Anyway,' he added, 'as far as I'm concerned, the thing that matters is that we beat 'em to it – such as it is – and that's one thing they can't undo.'

'No,' Troon nodded in agreement, 'there's nothing they can do about that.'

The two of them turned as if by common consent to look out of the window.

The prospect there was an average Venusian day. The

Venus

sky was simply a luminous white mist. Visibility was that within a layer of thin cloud, changing range quite rapidly as the mist drove along in a twenty-mile-an-hour wind. Most of the time one could see the sparse, high reeds that began forty yards away from the dome. They were slightly bent, and rippled in the wind like stiff hairs. Now and then the mist cleared enough for some minutes to reveal the tall, astonishingly flexible trees that someone had named feathertops, swinging back and forth in great arcs, two hundred yards away. The ground itself, both near and further, was covered with a matting of pale succulent tendrils, the Venusian equivalent of grass. Even at its clearest, it was not a view to inspire. Almost a monochrome study; shadowless, with only here and there a fleshy stalk showing a faint flush of pink, or a slight tinting of green to break the monotony of pallor. And over all, and all the time, there was the mist condensing; drops of water running down the etiolated stems, showers of them torn from the plants by sudden gusts of wind, endless rivulets of them trickling down the window-panes.

'It's all very well for us,' Arthur remarked. 'We've been financed to do what we wanted to do – make the first successful landing. Now, as far as I'm concerned, anybody can have it, and welcome.'

Troon shook his head.

'We weren't financed just to make a record, Arthur – nor just to give it away again. Part of our contract is to hold on to it.'

'Maybe if your Cousin Jayme could see what it's like he'd think again,' Arthur suggested.

'Not Jayme,' said Troon. 'He knows what he's doing, always did. The trouble is that, like his old man, he has such big ideas that you only see bits of them. No, he's satisfied, he's pleased.'

The Outward Urge

Arthur Dogget looked out of the window again, and shook his head.

'If he's pleased with this, there must be a lot more to it than we can see,' he said.

'I've no doubt. He and his old man are campaigners in a big way – kind of civilian field-marshals, and with complete confidence in themselves. The old man was never a bit impressed by the mere size of a job he took on, so he always kept his head – Jayme's the same way.'

'One of the things I've never understood,' Arthur said, 'is how a cousin of yours, and an Aussie citizen, comes to have a Brazzie name like Jayme Gonveia?'

'Oh, that isn't too difficult. When my grandfather, Geoffrey Trunho, died on the first expedition to Mars, he left three children: Anna, George, and Geoffrey, my father, who was born either posthumously, or at least after his father reached Mars. My Aunt Anna subsequently married one Henriques Polycarpo Gonveia – old man Gonveia, in fact – she emigrated with him to Australia, and Jayme is their son.

'Now, Jayme's grandfather Gonveia was a friend of *my* grandfather's, and when my grandfather failed to return from Mars, it was this Grandpa Gonveia who did most of the agitation for a second Martian expedition. In the end he got together a group who put up half the money for it, and shamed the Brazilian government into finding the rest. And his highly speculative share in the success of the expedition there in 2101 was half of the exclusive rights to any botanical finds. To everyone's surprise, some were actually made, along the bottom of the *canali* rifts, and he promptly bought the other fellow out of the half-share.

'For about twenty years his experts grew, developed, and adapted the seeds and plants, and then, as a result, Grandpa Gonveia and his two sons and daughter set out to conquer the world's deserts – which they are still doing.

Venus

João, the eldest son, took North Africa for his territory; Beatriz went to China, and my Uncle Henriques went off, as I said, to Australia.

'Anna's brother, my Uncle George, stayed in Brazil, and his son, Jorge Trunho, is a Commander in the Space Force there.

'My own father was sent to Australia to school, and then to São Paulo University. After taking his degree, he returned to Australia, married the daughter of a shipowner there, and was soon sent to manage his father-in-law's office in Durban. At the time of the Second African Rising, when the Africans threw out the Indians, he was accidentally killed in a riot. My mother, left with me, still a small baby, went home to live in Australia where she changed our name back to its original form of Troon.'

'I see – but it doesn't really explain how your cousin Jayme comes to be involved in this business. I'd have thought he'd be much too busy reclaiming deserts.'

'Not while his old man is still in the chair. They're too much of a kind. After he had had a year or so of the desert-blossoming business Jayme could see a lot of will-clashing ahead, so he started putting his main interest into other things. Well, I suppose that, what with the Gonveia strain and the Troon strain together, it was more or less a natural that he should get to thinking about space. He hasn't the Troon urge to get out into space; the Gonveia strain is stronger – he only wants to operate it – and the more he looked at space, lying out here with nobody doing anything about it, the more it irked him. After a bit, he got his old man interested, too, and then other people – which is why we're here today.'

'Until the Brazzies arrive to throw us, and his interests, out,' Arthur put in.

Troon shook his head.

133

The Outward Urge

'Don't you believe it. Jayme isn't the kind that gets thrown out – nor's the old man. I'd put the old man down as the richest, as well as the most valuable, immigrant Australia ever had; and there must be a goodish part of the Gonveia family fortune sunk in this. No, take it from me, they both know what they're doing.'

'I hope you're right. The Brazzy in the street must be tearing mad now he's heard about it – he's pretty proud of that "Space is a Province of Brazil" stuff.'

'True enough – even though he'd have more to be proud of if he'd done more about it. All the same, when you look at the difference the Gonveia family has made to the face of the earth with the hundreds of thousands of square miles of deserts they've salvaged, I think they're a good bet.'

'Well, I hope you're right. Things'll be a lot less sticky for us if you are,' Arthur Dogget replied.

Presently, when Arthur had gone off, leaving him alone, Troon looked at the message again, and wondered how his cousin was handling things back on Earth.

His thoughts returned to a day three years ago when a small private aircraft, dead on its appointed time, had hovered over his house, and then put down on his landing-lawn.

Out of it had emerged Jayme Gonveia, a large, active young man in a white suit, white hat, and blue silk shirt, looking rather too big to have fitted into the craft that had brought him. For a moment he had stood beside the machine, looking round George Troon's estate, noting the carefully spaced, thick-limbed Martian-derived trees that were something like spineless cacti, and the no less carefully arranged bushes of complementary kinds, examining the mesh of wiry grass beneath his feet, and the blades of wider-leafed grass coming up, sparsely as yet, through it. George, as he

Venus

approached, could see that, somewhat cheerlessly institutional as the calculated precision of the prospect appeared at present, Jayme was approving of it.

'Not doing badly,' he had greeted George. 'Five years?'

'Yes,' said George. 'Five years and three months now, from the bare sand.'

'Water good?'

'Adequate.'

Jayme nodded. 'In another three years you'll be starting real trees. In twenty you'll have a landscape, and a climate. Should do nicely. We've just developed a better grass than this. Grows faster, binds better. I'll tell them to send you some seed.'

They walked towards the house, across a patio, and into a large, cool room.

'I'm sorry Dorothea's away,' said George. 'She's gone to Rio for a couple of weeks. Dull for her here, I'm afraid.'

Jayme nodded again.

'I know. They get impatient. The first stages of reclamation aren't exciting. Is she a Brazilophile?'

'No – not really,' George told him. 'But you know how it is. Rio is lights, music, dresses, centre of the world and all that. It recharges her batteries. We usually go a couple of times a year. Occasionally she goes on her own. She's plenty of friends there.'

'Sorry to miss her,' said his cousin.

'She'll be sorry not to have seen you. Quite a time since you met,' George responded.

'Nevertheless,' said Jayme, 'it does make it a little easier to talk confidential business.'

George, in the act of approaching the drink-cupboard, turned round and looked at his cousin with a lifted eyebrow.

'Business?' he remarked. 'Since when am I supposed to

have known anything about business? And what sort of business?'

'Oh, just the usual Troon sort – space,' said Jayme.

George returned with bottles, glasses, and syphon, and set them down carefully.

' "Space",' he reminded his cousin, ' "Space is a Province of Brazil." '

'But it is also a kind of madness in the blood of the Troons,' Jayme replied.

'Now put under restraint for all of us – except, I suppose, for Jorge Trunho.'

'Suppose there were an escape-route?'

'I should be interested. Say on.'

Jayme Gonveia leant back in his chair.

'I have by now,' he said, 'grown more than a little tired of this "Province of Brazil" bluff. It is time it was called.'

'Bluff?' exclaimed George.

'Bluff,' Jayme repeated. 'Brazil has had it easy. She's been sitting on the top of the world so long that she thinks she's there for good, as a provision of nature. She's going soft. In the chaos that followed the Northern War she worked, and worked hard, to put herself on top; and since then, there have been no challengers to keep her on her toes. She's just sat back over the matter of space, too. When she first proclaimed it a Province she reclaimed the damaged Satellites, and made three of them spaceworthy again, and she took over and improved the old British Moon Station. But since then . . . !

'Well, look at the record. . . . Nothing at all until Grandpa Trunho's unlucky Mars expedition in 2094. There wouldn't have been a second expedition there unless Grandpa Gonveia and his pals had pressed for it in 2101. The third, in 2105, was financed entirely by public subscription, and since then no one has set foot on the place.

Venus

'They abandoned the smallest Satellite back in 2080. In 2115 they abandoned another, keeping only Primeira in commission. In 2111 a newspaper and radio campaign on the neglect of space forced them into sending the first Venus expedition – and a shabby affair that was, scandalously ill-equipped; never heard from once it had entered the Venus atmosphere, and no wonder. Ten years later they allowed a learned society to send another ship there – by subscription again. When that, too, disappeared, they just gave up. In the twenty years since then nothing further has been done, nothing at all. They've spent just enough to keep Primeira and the Moon Station habitable, so that they can hog their monopoly of space and, if necessary, threaten the rest of us from there, and that's all. What a record!'

'Far from admirable,' agreed George Troon. 'And so – ?'

'And so they are going to pay the usual penalty of neglect. Someone else is going to step in.'

'Meaning Jayme Gonveia?'

'With a kind of syndicate I've got together. It's unofficial, of course. The Australian government just can't afford to know anything about it. Support for any idea of the kind would definitely be an unfriendly act towards the Brazilian people. However, we naturally had need of designers, and of the use of yards to build the ships, so that there is – well – a little more than a liaison between us and certain government departments. Nominally, however, it has to be an adventure with a rather old-world title – privateering.'

George kept the excitement that was speeding up his pulses carefully imperceptible.

'Well, well,' he said, in a tone that matched his cousin's. 'Would I be astray in suspecting that there is a part for me in these plans?'

'So perceptive of you, George. Yes, I remember you as a boy on the subject of space; the veritable Troon obsession.

The Outward Urge

As they never outgrow it, I am assuming that you still hear the "thin gnat-voices calling"?'

'I've had to muffle them, Jayme, but they are still there.'

'I thought so, George. So now let me tell you about the job,' Jayme had said.

A year later, the *Aphrodite*, with a complement of ten, including George Troon in command, had set out. She was a new kind of ship, for she had a new kind of task – Venus in one leap, with no help from Satellite or Moon Station. As such, she was devoid of all unnecessary weight: victualled and found only for one voyage and a few weeks more; everything beyond bare necessities was to follow her in supply-rockets.

A supply-rocket (or 'shuttle', or 'crate') could be built for a fraction of the cost of a manned rocket. With living-quarters, insulation, air supply, water-purifying system, and all the rest of the human needs eliminated, the payload could be over fifty per cent higher. Launching, too, was more economical; a shuttle could be given a ground-boost and a quick step-boost producing an acceleration several times greater than a human cargo could survive. Once launched and locked on to its target, it would continue to travel by inertia until it should pick up the coded radio signals that would check and take charge of it. There was no more difficulty in directing a supply-rocket to Venus than in aiming it for a Satellite or for the moon, and no more power was needed to get it there – though it would require extra fuel for a safe landing against the planetary pull.

The question of supplies, therefore, raised few difficulties. The problems arose over the key-ship, the manned *Aphrodite*, for she must take off under full load, sustain her crew for the voyage, and, above all, be manoeuvrable enough in atmosphere to choose her landing when she should arrive.

Venus

It was the last proviso that called for modified design. Both the previous expeditions were known to have entered the Venus atmosphere. It was after that that something fatal had befallen them, and the general opinion among spacemen was that neither had proved sufficiently manoeuvrable to pick, and, if necessary, to change its choice of, landing-place with accuracy. On a vapour-bound planet where inspection could not be visual until the last moments, that was essential.

Many years ago it had been supposed that Venus was entirely, or almost entirely, water-covered. That had later given way to the theory that the perpetual clouds were not vaporous, but were formed of dust swept up from an arid surface by constant fierce winds. Several times since then opinions had swung this way and that between the two extremes until there was general acceptance of the view that the planet was probably waterlogged, but scarcely likely to lack land masses entirely. Radar, however, would not be able to distinguish accurately between marshland and solid ground – or even, with certainty, between either and floating weed-beds, should such exist. Infra-red would tell more, but from a comparatively low altitude. It might well be that the true nature of the ground would be indiscernible above a few hundred feet, and it was imperative, therefore, that a ship which discovered itself to be descending upon a mudbank, or a morass, should have the ability to draw off and search for better ground. It was a problem that had not occurred with Earth landings where a ship was brought in by an alliance of radio and electronic control, nor had it arisen on Mars, with its dry surface and normally perfect visibility.

In the event, the last stage of the *Aphrodite*'s journey had proved the worth of the designers' trouble. Had she not been able to cruise at moderate altitude in search of a

The Outward Urge

landing-place, there would have been an end of her. The cruise gave her the opportunity to discover that the proportion of land to sea over the area she covered was extremely small, and none of it was the high, firm ground she sought.

At last, Troon decided to return to the largest island so far observed – a low-lying mass about one hundred and fifty miles long and a hundred miles across at its widest, misted over, and sodden under continuous rain. Even then it had been difficult to find a suitable landing area; hard to tell whether the monotonous grey-white vegetation they saw below was low-growing bushes, or densely packed tree-tops; impossible to know what sort of ground lay beneath it. One could do no more than make a guess from the apparent configuration of the ground.

Troon had made six unsuccessful attempts to land the ship. On two of them she got as far as touching the mud, and starting to sink into it, before blasting free again. At the seventh try, however, the tripod supports had squelched through only two or three inches of mud before they found a firm bottom. Then, at last, Troon had been able to switch off, and stagger over to his bunk, past caring or wanting to know anything more about the planet he had reached.

The *Aphrodite*'s landing took place two weeks ahead of conjunction. A week later they had picked up the signal of the first supply-rocket, switched on contact, and put it into a spiral. They lost it for an hour or two when it was on the other side of the planet on its first circuit, but picked it up again as it came round, and held it thereafter. It was brought in and landed successfully in a roughly surveyed area a mile or so to the south of the ship.

Of the seven that followed it in the course of the next two weeks, only Number 5 gave trouble. In the final stages of descent she developed a fault which cut out the main drive, and dropped her like a stone for two hundred feet.

Venus

She split open as she hit, but luckily it had been possible to salvage most of her contents. The unloading priority had been the Dome from Number 2 rocket; it was badly needed to get them out of the cramped cabin of the *Aphrodite*, and give them shelter from the eternal rain and drizzle into a place where there would be room to live and work and protect the stores. Even before it was fully ready, however, there had come a message from Jayme, saying laconically:

'They're on to you, George. You have 584 days, or a little less, to get ready for them.'

'They', it quickly became clear, meant only certain official circles in Brazil, and their knowledge was severely restricted. A public admission that an expedition had not only made an unauthorized incursion into the Brazilian 'Province of Space', but had stolen a march on its nominal administrators by achieving the first successful landing on Venus, would involve not only the Space Department, but the whole government in a serious loss of face. The evident intention was to avoid publicity, while counter measures were prepared, possibly in the hope that if the secret could be kept until a Brazilian expedition had been dispatched at the next conjunction there might be no need of the admission at all.

Absence of publicity suited both parties for the present. So long as it lasted, no awkward representations could be made to the Australian government, and no overt, or even covert, reprisals taken. Meanwhile both of them employed the interlude which the laws of planetary motion imposed.

On Venus, once the essentials of the Dome were erected, the entire party busied itself with collecting, photographing, preserving, and crating specimens of Venusian air, water, soil, rock, plants, seeds, and insect-type life, working against time to get at least these preliminary, and as yet unclassified, specimens loaded aboard the emptied Number 2 supply-

The Outward Urge

rocket, and dispatched as soon as possible towards the now receding Earth. Only when that had been accomplished did they relax, and, turning their attention to the other shuttles, set about making the Dome into as comfortable a habitation as possible.

Back in Rio, the higher levels of the Space Force pulled schemes for Venusian expeditions out of their pigeon-holes, called in technicians, and started to get down to the task of creating a commando which must be ready, not only to reach Venus by the time of the next conjunction, but to take police action when it should arrive.

When the matter of assigning personnel arose, it was almost inevitable that Space-Commander Jorge Manoel Trunho should be among those chosen. His qualifications and record were first-class, and his family's history and tradition would have made failure to include him invidious.

In Sydney, Jayme Gonveia, through his own peculiar channels, received the news of the appointment with satisfaction. There was a place in his plans for Commander J. M. Trunho.

The Satellite, Primeira, now alerted, detected Number 2 supply-rocket in the course of its return journey to Earth, and inquired whether it should intercept with a guided missile. A hurried council called in Rio was divided in its opinions. The members could not know that the object detected was simply a freighter. It *might* be the expedition returning. It was true that messages originating upon Venus were still being picked up, in an as yet unbroken code, but they *might* be dummy messages, originating from an automatic transmitter left there as a bluff. If the returning rocket were to be summarily blown to bits, and then turned out to have contained the expedition, or even a part of it, somebody would certainly give the matter publicity, and the public reaction would be bad. The government would be

Venus

reviled for an act scarcely to be distinguished from murder, and the victims would very likely become heroes overnight. In the end, therefore, Primeira was instructed to make no attack, but to continue observation, and home stations were ordered to be ready to track the object as it approached the Earth. This they did, but had the misfortune to lose it somewhere over the Pacific Ocean, and no more was heard of it.

Thereafter, for more than a year, all parties had worked secretly, and without alarms.

Now that the cat was, at last, publicly out of the bag it caused political ructions in Rio, but made little practical difference. Not even to appease the wrath of the Brazilian people could the conjunction of planets be hastened. Time had been short enough anyway, and, whatever ministers might say in speeches, preparations could only go ahead as planned.

In Sydney, Jayme Gonveia boarded a Brazil-bound aircraft in order to study reactions at their centre. It was a stage that called for careful observation and assessment, with perhaps a little influence thrown in at critical moments. His only surprise was that the breakdown of security had not come sooner. A leakage he had expected, but he had not foreseen the source of it, and hoped that by the time George Troon returned the details would have been forgotten.

For Dorothea, Mrs George Troon, after a year of a pre-occupied husband, followed by more than a year of grass-widowhood tediously spent in the slowly regenerating wilderness that was her home, was in the habit of making periodical visits to Rio to break up the depression induced by these things. Taken by friends one night to a party which she found unamusing, she had attempted to improve it by several glasses of iced aguadente and passion-fruit, dashed with quinine and bitters. Her intention of raising her spirits had somehow gone wrong, and she had lifted, instead, the sluices of self-pity. She became woefully the neglected wife. And though in the course of lamenting this, she did not actually mention her husband's whereabouts, it became clear that she had not seen him for some little time – clear enough to catch the attention of one Agostinho Tarope, a fellow-guest who happened also to be a columnist on the *Diario do São Paulo*. It occurred to Agostinho that a prolonged absence of a member of the Troon family could have interesting implications, and if his subsequent inquiries did not produce many hard facts, he collected enough indications to convince himself that it was worth taking a risk with some pointed comment. Other papers pounced upon, and inflated, his speculations. Nobody was able to produce George Troon to refute the rumours, and the row was on. . . .

The Brazzy in the street was, as Arthur Dogget had suggested, tearing mad. He turned out in large numbers, carrying banners which proclaimed Space to be a Province of Brazil, and demanded action against Australian aggression. Replying to an official approach, the Australian government denied any knowledge of the matter, but undertook to look into the rumours, while pointing out that Australia was a free country of free citizens.

Political and official circles in Brazil were far from unanimous. Factions started to form. Some held the forthright chauvinist view of holding on to space at any cost; others saw it as a regrettable expense, but a strategic necessity; one group considered it a waste of money to maintain stations and a force which could bring no return. Strong complaints about the lack of enterprise in the development of space began to be heard again.

The Space Force itself was split several ways. Those at the top, and previously in the know, were already resentful at being shaken out of a comfortable routine, and reacted with bluster to the newspaper comments on the inefficiency of the Service. The youngest stratum of officers and men began to look forward to action and excitement in the defence of space. Among the men with longer service, however, there was variety of opinion. Many of those who had joined for the great adventure of exploring space, only to find themselves stagnating for years in sentry duty, showed a cynicism little short of subversive. Plenty of disillusioned voices could be heard asking: 'Why stop 'em? All we've done out there for a hundred years is play dog-in-the-manger – and it'll be no better if we do chuck 'em out. If there are others ready to have a shot at really doing a job out there, then let 'em, I say. And good luck to 'em.'

It was to this stratum of opinion that Jayme Gonveia was giving his most careful attention at the moment....

Meanwhile, the party on Venus had found its forbearance severely tested.

Once the Dome had been made comfortable, the three jet-platforms assembled, and the island mapped by infra-red photography, exploration, in its wider sense, had virtually come to an end. The land was found to be monotonously low-lying, with a backbone of raised ground which at its highest points barely exceeded one hundred feet. Much of the coast was hard to determine, for it shelved gradually into a tideless sea in great stretches of swamps and marsh, and the weeds growing out of the muddy water had little to distinguish them from those that covered the saturated land. Animate life on the island was restricted to insects, a few wandering crustaceans not unsimilar to spider-crabs which seldom came far from the shore, and a few lunged fish, apparently in the process of becoming amphibians. In the sea there was plenty of life, large and small, but the coastal marshes cut off all surface approach, and the disturbance

The Outward Urge

caused by the jets made it all but impossible to net specimens from hovering platforms.

Cautious descents were made in various parts of the island to take samples. Landing on the lower ground was usually out of the question, and even on the higher slopes it was risky. The platform had to hang cautiously just above the growths while one member of its crew probed with a long rod. With luck, there might be rock a few inches below the surface, and it could put down. Far more often there was a bed of dangerous mud where the probe would go feet deep into a mush made by generations of rotting plants, discovering no bottom at all. So there, too, most of the specimen-taking had to be conducted with scoops wielded from the platforms.

'A fiery hell,' Dogget had proclaimed, 'seems a nice clean conception when you compare it with the stinking, rotting slime under the goddamned, never-ending rain in this place.'

Any exploration beyond the bounds of the island was out of the question, for observation had already shown how rare land was, and the platforms were not equal to long-range travel. There was, therefore, no disposition whatever to risk taking them out over the uncharted seas.

The biologists of the party had far the best of it. Poring over sections through microscopes gave them endless interest.

Once the shuttles had been unloaded there was little temptation to go outside the Dome for anything other than a specimen collecting expedition; inside, kept dry and comfortable by a desiccating plant, there was increasing boredom for all but the four biologists. They remained happily busy and, by degrees, the rest drifted into lending them a hand, and into becoming biologists, or at least biologists' assistants, themselves. Troon observed the development with approval.

Venus

'Good,' he said, 'it saves me getting round to the cliché of "They also serve...." I'd hate that, because it's not really the statement it appears to be; more often it is an indication that the speaker is getting troubled about morale. So anything for some interest, even if it is only water bugs. Conjunction is a bit too infrequent. Five hundred and eighty-four days is a long time to be stuck on a mudbank.'

'I'd doubt if the Brazzies could mount an expedition in less, anyway,' Dogget said, 'or whether, if they knew what this place is like, they'd bother to send one at all.'

'Oh, they would. Matter of principle. As long as we are here, space is not entirely a Province of Brazil. Besides, it may not turn out to be quite as useless as it seems to us at present.'

'H'm,' Arthur Dogget said, dubiously. 'Anyway, it was a bit of intolerable bombast ever to claim it. Space should be there for anyone who is willing to explore and exploit it.'

Troon grinned.

'Spoken like a true Briton. Just what the English said about the undiscovered world when there was the same sort of bombastic assumption over that. In the days of real Papal dictatorship, Alexander VI reckoned the whole place was his to allocate, so in an open-handed way he gave the Portuguese the East, and the Spaniards the West. And what happened? The very next year that arrangement came unstuck, and the Portuguese enterprisingly claimed the whole of South America, and six years later Cabral took possession of Brazil for them.'

'Did he, now? And what did the Pope have to say to that?'

'He wasn't in a position to say anything. That particular Spiritual Servant happened to be a Borgia, and died of a bowl of poisoned wine he had prepared for a friend. But the point is this, claiming things is rather in the Portuguese blood.

Vasco da Gama claimed India for them, but they held only Goa; and of South America, they held only Brazil – until they lost it. Now their descendants claim all space, but hold only a Satellite Station and the moon. Their earlier grandiose claims did not keep the British, and the Dutch, and the rest, out of undeveloped territories, and there's no good reason why the present ones should.'

'H'm,' said Arthur again. 'Times have changed, though. We've got here. But I don't see how, even if the place were worth hanging on to, we could keep up any regular communications between Earth and this gob of mud – not with guided missiles out hunting for us each trip. I'd like to know the real plan. Sometimes I get a nasty feeling that we could be – just bait. . . .'

'In a way, of course, we are,' Troon admitted. 'The existing situation had to be cracked open some way. I think this is a pretty good one. As the matter stands now, a lot of people in Brazil will be calling us pirates and other, ruder things – though not all of them, by any means. But what about the rest of the world? They'll be taking a very different view of it. I don't mind betting we are popular heroes now, in most places – and on two counts: one, that we have made a successful landing here at last; and the other, that we've wiped the Brazzy eye. Everybody will be delighted over that – which will be the chief reason that the Brazzies are wild. What is more, it puts them in a spot. They have foreign relations to preserve, so they can't just drop a bomb on us, for they would then appear as the big, crude bully; they'd earn world-wide hostile contempt, and very likely plenty at home, too. In fact, if they actually turn any kind of weapons on us at all, they'll be in for a lot of opprobrium. So it looks as if the only way they can handle it, without losing even more prestige than they have already, is to capture us and run us as ignominiously as possible out of what they claim to be their territory – being careful, on account of public relations, to do us as little physical damage as possible.

'Very well, then. They will arrive with the intention of netting us. But we are here first. We can make preparations for that. *We* have at least as good a chance of netting *them*, if we work it right. And that's what we've got to do.'

'And when we have?' Arthur asked.

'I'm not sure. But at least we shall have hostages.'

'Your cousin Jayme must have a plan for the next stage?'

'I don't doubt it. But that is as far as he is telling at present.'

'I just hope your degree of confidence in him is justified.'

'My dear Arthur, a great deal of money has been sunk in this affair – including a large part of the Gonveia family fortune. It is evident that cleverer men, with more to lose than you and I, are satisfied that Jayme knows what he's doing.'

'I hope you're right – I'd just like to be able to see more of the picture, that's all.'

'We shall. I'm willing to bet that the overall strategy is being taken good care of, from the little I know of it. But the local tactics are our affair, of course, and it seems to me the best thing we can do is to work out several plans to suit different circumstances. When we know more about how they are going to tackle it, and what their equipment is, we can fill in the details of the most suitable plans. At present our information on their plans is still pretty slim, but we shall get more. In the meantime, my idea of preparing a reception for them is this....'

The Brazilians, being under no obligation to make their Venus-bound lift direct from Earth, had no intention of trying it. The Satellite, Primeira, offered them a means of

The Outward Urge

starting and building up speed without the drag of gravity and, naturally, they made use of that. Gone, therefore, even a few weeks after the first intelligence of the Troon expedition's presence on Venus, were Primeira's leisurely days when the only interruptions of her comfortable lethargy were the supply-shuttles and the monthly relief rockets. Orders started to pour in. Sections of the Satellite that had been closed-off and put out of commission years ago were opened up, examined, tested, repaired where necessary, and made habitable again. Quantities of supplies came up in shuttles and, presently, technicians followed them. Soon long cylinders of a new ballistic type, containers of air, water, stores, fuel, and the rest were arriving, to be captured and tethered electronically about the station. Later on came sections of larger shuttles. Engineers in space-suits emerged from Primeira and jetted themselves across the void to start assembling them. In a few months, the whole neighbourhood of the Satellite was littered with floating masses of metal and containers of all shapes and sizes, gradually being drawn together and bolted, welded, and sealed into comprehensible shapes. The work went on continuously in shifts, with artificial lights blazing during the brief 'nights' in the Earth's shadow, until gradually the chaos was tidied into the form of five large new shuttles. Activity then became less spectacular while the engineers worked inside them, fitting the new hulks with their electronic circuits, linking the remote-controls to the main drive, and stabilizing and correcting jets; testing, adjusting, and readjusting the gear's responses to radio signals which would be their only pilots.

While that was still going on, the ballistic cylinders were opened, and again the area was littered with space-suited men gently propelling cases of all shapes and sizes towards one or another of the shuttles, for stowage. The ballistic cylinders themselves were expendable – it would have cost more to get one safely back to Earth and recondition it than to make a new one, so that when they were emptied a charge was clamped on to them, and they were dispatched to crash harmlessly among the lunar crags, where they could no longer be a hazard to navigation.

The work went well, and in spite of setbacks, it was completed a full month ahead of schedule. The area was then clear. The five fully-loaded shuttles, linked by cables, hung in a bunch, revolving about the Satellite at a range of twenty miles and linked to it by radio beam. The Satellite itself, the intricate machine that had grown up from the first of all the space-stations, kept smoothly on its orbit, with two small rocket-ships in attendance, waiting.

'They are using shuttles, as I told you,' Jayme Gonveia informed Troon. 'They have, however, improved on our method – presumably because, had they to await the arrival of their shuttles as you did of yours, they would be in a weak position and unable to take any action against you until the shuttles should arrive. The idea they have adopted, therefore, is one of unified control whereby they and their shuttles will travel together and arrive simultaneously. The whole group is intended to handle as one ship. This means that you must be prepared to take very swift action before they have a chance to deploy . . .'

The key-ship, the *Santa Maria*, came up two weeks before the calculated starting date, and hove to, hanging in space a mere mile or so from Primeira. She had left Earth with only five men aboard; the rest of her full complement of twenty were awaiting her on the Satellite. With her arrival, activity broke out again. Figures emerged from Primeira's locks, some of them jetting across the gap immediately, others manoeuvring containers out of the dock-doors and guiding

The Outward Urge

them into a drift towards the ship. Once more there began a process of testing and checking, which, with the provisioning and final fitting-out, continued in shifts for a week.

Inspected and passed at last, the *Santa Maria* moved off a few miles. The cluster of the five waiting shuttles was brought closer and broken up. Each of them was urged and juggled into aproximately its proper relation to the rest.

When the last was placed, the small tug-shells and thrusters drew off and made back to Primeira, leaving on each shuttle a party of only four space-suited men, linked together by lines and equipped with portable jet-tubes to steady their charges and correct drift. In the centre, roughly equidistant from all five shuttles, the *Santa Maria* waited. Aboard her, Capitão João Camarello and his first officer, Commander Jorge Trunho, watched the tugs draw clear of the area.

'Ready, shuttles?' the Capitão asked.

A man on each shuttle acknowledged.

'Good,' approved the Capitão. 'Keep ready. We shall make contact with you in exactly ten minutes from ... *now.*'

The space-suited men clinging to the shuttles continued to check twist and drift in their charges as well as they could.

'Two minutes to alignment,' said the Capitão. 'Get clear of all tubes now, and check your short safety lines. No trouble? Fine. One minute to go now. ... Thirty seconds. ... Ten seconds. ... *Now!*'

The Chief Electronics Officer pressed his first key.

Little jets of flame broke from the steering tubes of the shuttles. Each turned over, rolled, and twisted, swinging round to align itself with the parent ship, firing more small jets to correct and steady the over-swing. Presently, all were lying in exactly the same orientation, with their main

Venus

driving tubes pointed towards the gleaming crescent of the Earth.

'Phase One completed. All well?' inquired the Capitão.

One after another the men tethered to the shuttles reported. He went on:

'Positioning will take place in two minutes from ... *now!*'

The Electronics Officer regarded the hand of the clock, pressed his second key, and turned his attention to a small screen in front of him. Outside, more little twinkling bursts came from the shuttles; on the screen, small illuminated figures started to drift very slowly. Presently, the white figure 4 turned green, and ceased to drift.

'Number Four fixed, sir,' he reported.

The Capitão glanced at the screen.

'Good. Use that as the axis.'

Gradually the other figures changed the direction of their drift. One after another they too turned green. As the last one altered, the Officer reported.

'Formation complete and locked, sir.'

The Capitão lifted the microphone.

'Good work, boys, and thank you. Commander, you can take your men home now. We shall test control.'

The men in space-suits unhooked, kicked off into the void, then levelled their hand-tubes, and set themselves scudding through emptiness towards the Satellite. When they reached it, they were able to look back and see the pattern of their operation complete.

The *Santa Maria* lay relatively motionless. About her, each at a distance of more than two miles, hung the shuttles, at the angles of a huge pentagon. Invisible proximity beams linked them all, each to the *Santa Maria* in the middle and to both of its neighbours. Occasionally one or another would show a brief twinkle of flame as the automatic gear cut in to correct the least loss of position.

The Outward Urge

Six Earth-days later, the personnel on Primeira collected round the stationary screen in their spinning home to watch the start. The farewells and good wishes were over, and they watched in silence. A voice aboard the *Santa Maria* came through the loudspeaker, counting the seconds, then Capitão Camarello's order: 'Fire!'

From the main tubes of the *Santa Maria*, and from those of all the five shuttles, belched jets of flame, quickly growing fiercer. The whole formation began to move as one. The blast of the driving tubes grew whiter, and fiercer still. In a few minutes the expedition was gone and, to mark it, a new constellation hung in a bright pentagon against the jet-black sky....

'*Of course* we keep up radio communication,' Troon explained patiently, 'and *of course* they'll locate us by it. This is a showdown. It's no damn good their landing in some other part of this pestiferous planet where neither of us can get at the other, is it? The nearer to us they land, the better, because the sooner we can reach them. But God knows what sort of a mess their landing's going to be. We had quite enough trouble in getting just one ship down safely.'

'As I understand it,' said Arthur, 'the whole unit works on a kind of servo system by which, whatever the manned key-ship does, the rest do the same. That must be so, I think; the elaborations and complications of five men in one ship controlling five shuttles independently while that ship is descending are beyond contemplation. Therefore, the intention must be to land in the same formation they travel in – a pentagon; though I suppose they may be able to contract or expand its size a bit. That being so, all their attention will have to be concentrated on the safe landing of the key-ship, and the shuttles must more or less take their chance. Those chaps certainly can't know what they're in for. You *might* bring off a trick like that fairly neatly on a dead flat prairie, but not on a mud pie. My betting is that it will be only luck if *one* of their shuttles stays upright, and most likely that all of them will sink in the swamps.'

'We can't be bothered about that,' Troon told him. 'What we have to concentrate on is being as close as we can to the key-ship when she comes down, and without having any of the shuttles coming down on top of us. It would help if we knew what distances they intend to keep. We'd better get on to Jayme again, and see if he has any information on the landing drill.'

Excellent as Jayme's information service was, it could not help there. Any decision to expand or contract the pentagon formation must obviously, he pointed out, be left to the captain's discretion. His sources continued, however, to give reliable information on the expedition's progress, and as its E.T.A. drew near, the radar was set searching for it beyond the Venus cloud cover. The formation was first faintly detected at a great height, still moving fast, and presumably closing on a spiral. Troon promptly dispatched a message announcing its approach. On its second circuit, still at a considerable distance, but travelling more slowly, it had altered direction, from which he judged that the point of origin of his message had been plotted.

'Make ready,' he ordered. 'They ought to be down next time.'

The party checked that its weapons and supplies in waterproof covers were aboard the three jet-platforms, then they climbed into their space-suits, as the best form of protection against the never-ending rain outside, and waited, with their helmets handy.

At last the formation showed up on the screen, seen now from a different angle, travelling slowly in from the north at a mere twenty-five thousand feet. All six ships had tilted

The Outward Urge

almost to the vertical, but the pentagon formation was still perfect, and now in the same plane with the surface of the ground. As they came closer, standing on their main drives they showed simply as a pattern of circular spots which drifted almost to the centre of the screen.

The party in the Dome put on its helmets, and made for platforms, leaving a single man at the radar. He hooked up a microphone, and his voice reached them all.

'Key-ship east-north-east, estimate five miles. Separation from servo ships, estimate one mile. Appears constant.'

The platforms rose a little and skimmed out of the locks, climbing on a gentle slant.

'Don't bother about the shuttles unless the separation alters. Concentrate on the key-ship,' Troon told the operator.

'Right, George. Rate of descent slow and cautious. I'd say around twelve hundred a minute. Now a little under eighteen thousand. Steady and vertical.'

The platforms sped on, travelling a few feet above the tops of the trees which rose out of the tangle of pallid, slimy growths that hid the ground. Presently, Troon brought his to a halt, and sent the other two out on the flanks. Hanging there, with the fronds of the feather-top trees swinging across just beneath him, he switched on the outside microphone, and heard for the first time the roar of the rockets overhead. The thunder of six rocket-ships descending at once was almost unnerving. He switched off again, and the three of them stood peering anxiously into the clouds above. A few minutes seemed a long time.

'Eight thousand,' said the radar man. And a little later: 'Five thousand.'

One could hear the noise now through the helmet, and feel the buffeting of the sound waves. A man on one of the other platforms exclaimed suddenly: 'There's one of them!'

Almost at the same moment Troon's neighbour caught

his arm, and pointed up. Troon looked and saw a brilliant, diffused, reddish light with a quality of sunset, breaking through above them. He sent the platform swooping forward, out of harm's way.

The buffeting grew, until the platform was trembling with it. He could see four glows in the clouds now. The one behind, one ahead, two dimmer ones on either side, but all of them growing brighter. The platform began to sway as if the roaring billows of sound were tossing it.

'Under one thousand,' said the radar man's voice.

'They're lucky – dead lucky. Quite a bit of firm ground round here,' came Arthur's voice.

Troon did his best to look all ways at once. The flare behind was still the closest. He edged a little further away from it, and then kept his eyes on the one ahead; that, he calculated, must be that of the key-ship. All three men clung fast to their holds as the platform rocked.

It became barely possible to look at the brilliance. Hanging on with one hand, he raised the other in front of his helmet and peered through slits between his gloved fingers. At two hundred feet the flames were stabbing into the ground, and the steam was rising in thickening clouds, to blot everything. A moment later, there was nothing to be seen but a dazzling white nimbus, with its centre slowly growing more intense. Troon looked quickly round again; all about them was whitely shining steam. Then, suddenly, the noise stopped; the platform ceased to tremble; the vivid white spots in the steam died. In the abrupt silence of his helmet Troon asked:

'Arthur, have you marked the key-ship?'

'I reckon so, George.'

'You, Ted?'

'Pretty sure of her, George. I'll make certain when this steam lets up. She'll have ports. The others won't.'

'Well, both of you stay where you are until you can be sure. Then find her airlock side, and close in to fifty yards.'

He edged his own platform forward. The air was clearing, but it was not possible to see the ship yet. She was still hidden somewhere in the cloud of steam vaporizing from the sodden ground, but it seemed fairly certain that her landing, at any rate, had been successful, whatever might have happened to the shuttles.

Visibility gradually improved. Before long, he could see the outline of her top. Soon he could make out the upper part clearly enough to see the ports and be sure that she was the *Santa Maria*, and no unmanned shuttle. She was leaning a little, but not dangerously at present. He drove the platform forward towards the steam that still shrouded her base.

Gradually that thinned too. He was able to see that she had indeed been lucky in her landing-place, and the tripod foot on the tilt side showed no sign of sinking further. He took the platform down to a few feet above the ground, and a little closer. The ends of the ship's main driving tubes were still glowing, and the rain was vanishing into little steam puffs before it could actually touch them; the area directly beneath her was seared clear of vegetation, and muddy water was seeping back into it, steaming gently.

Troon brought his platform down to within inches of the ground, and steered it in between two of the tripod legs.

'Let it go!' he said.

His two companions unclipped the straps of a rectangular bale sealed into a waterproof cover, and tumbled it over the side to fall in the mud with a squelch. Skilfully Troon checked the upward bounce of the platform as it lost the weight; then he backed off, and sped away.

Venus

'Arthur? Ted? Have you located the airlock yet?'

'Arthur here. Yes, George. It's facing due south.'

'Good. Keep it covered. I'll be round there with you.'

He handed control of the platform over to one of his companions, and turned a knob on his helmet, putting his headset on to one of the Brazilian Space Force's intercom wavelengths. In Portuguese, he called:

'Troon calling! Troon calling! Troon calling Capitão Camarello.'

There was a short pause during which his platform approached Arthur's, and drew up beside it, then a voice replied:

'This is the *Santa Maria*, Spaceship of the Estados Unidos do Brazil, Capitão João Camarello.'

'*Bonos dias, Capitão*,' said Troon. 'And my felicitations, Senhor, upon your excellent landing.'

'*Muito obrigado*, Senhor Troon. And my congratulations to you upon your survival of the rigours of this singularly unattractive-looking planet. It is, however, my regrettable duty to inform you that, by order of the Congress of the United States of Brazil, you and your companions are under arrest, charged with violating the sovereignty of Brazilian territory. One hopes that you will recognize the situation and accept it.'

'Your message is not unexpected, Senhor,' Troon told him. 'But in return I must inform you that since the Brazilian claim to this territory rests neither on its discovery by Brazil, nor upon Brazil's prime establishment here, it cannot be considered to have any validity. I am therefore entitled on the grounds of your unauthorized landing to require that you and your crew should put yourselves under my orders. Until I have your assurance that this will be done, I cannot grant you permission to leave your ship.'

The Outward Urge

'Mr Troon, you have been informed, I do not doubt, of the strength of our expedition, so may I remind you that there are two of us to one of you – if, indeed, your party has survived intact the tribulations of such a detestable climate as this appears to be.

'That is quite true, Capitão Camarello, but *we* are not caught in a metal trap. Furthermore I ought, I think, to tell you that we have your airlock covered. And I must also warn you against an attempt to take off again, should it occur to you to look for a more hospitable landing area. There is, beneath you at this moment, a considerable bale of T.N.T. You cannot fire your drive without igniting it before you lift, whereupon it may do your ship considerable damage, and will certainly overturn her, thus making take-off impossible for you. Your situation, therefore, is awkward, Capitão.'

After a pause, the voice replied:

'Ingenious, Mr Troon. I will take your word for it. But at least we do not have to sit out in the rain in order to maintain our side of the impasse.'

'But neither do we, Senhor. Unless I receive your capitulation very shortly, we shall simply fix a wire cable round your ship in such a position as to prevent the outer door of your airlock from opening. We shall then be able to wait indefinitely, and in somewhat more comfort than yourselves, for your decision.'

Troon caught sight of Arthur Dogget signalling him from the next platform. He switched over to their usual wavelength. Arthur said:

'If he does agree – and I can't see that he's got any choice – what do we do with them, George? Keep 'em handcuffed all the time? After all, they're two to one, as he said. Why should he keep any agreement to surrender?'

'All right,' Troon told him. 'Just you wait a bit, and see.

Venus

We'll set down now to save power – but keep an eye on that door. Give it a bullet if it so much as moves.'

The three platforms descended carefully, seeking spots where the matting of growth was thick enough to keep them out of the mud, and waited. Troon switched back to the other wavelength, but a full hour passed before any sound could be heard on it; and then it was another voice that spoke:

'Hallo,' it said, 'George Troon?'

Troon acknowledged.

'Jorge Trunho here,' said the voice.

'I was hoping to hear from you, Cousin Jorge,' said Troon. 'What's the reply?'

'A change of authority,' Jorge Trunho told him. 'I have now taken command of this ship. With the exception of Capitão Camarello and four other men whom we have put under arrest, we are now willing to carry out your orders.'

'I am glad you appreciate that there was no sense in prolonging the situation,' said Troon, and issued his instructions. As he switched over, Arthur Dogget said:

'What goes on, George? I don't like this at all. It's a whole lot too easy.'

'You don't need to worry,' Troon told him. 'The Brazilian Space Force is riddled with young men who've been frustrated for years and know they're likely to stay that way as long as Brazil has the monopoly of space. They're over-ripe for a change. All that was needed was the opportunity, and someone to organize.'

Arthur considered.

'You mean – this was all fixed? You put 'em in a spot to give Trunho the chance to take over? You knew he would?'

'That was the plan, Arthur. The awkward spot made it easier for him to sway the undecided ones.'

The Outward Urge

'I see. All nicely arranged in advance – and by Cousin Jayme, I suppose?'

Troon nodded.

'Under his auspices, at any rate. I told you Cousin Jayme knows what he's doing.'

The slow twist on the *Santa Maria* was about to bring the sun into view, but before it could come searing through the port Arthur Dogget pushed the cover across and fixed it. He looked round the bare, tank-like compartment in which they were confined, then he pushed himself across to his acceleration-couch, fastened the straps to give some illusion of weight, and lay there frowning. At length, he said:

'What makes me kick myself – what really burns me up, is that I knew at the time it was all too damned easy – I even *said so*. God what a mug!'

Troon shook his head.

'It *should* have been easy – it was intended to be. That part of it would have gone just the way it did even if Jorge hadn't been double-crossing. The whole thing went quite according to plan, until he pulled that fast one when we got back to the Dome. It's no good blaming ourselves for trusting Jorge. We *had* to. Ten of us couldn't have kept twenty of them under restraint indefinitely. It was a calculated risk. Jayme was gambling on Cousin Jorge's Troon blood – that his spaceward urge would be greater than his loyalty to the Brazilian Space Force. Well, that was a bad bet – or was it? I'm still not quite sure. It may not have been loyalty. It could easily be that he was reckoning the chances differently. He *could* be calculating that after this shake-up the Brazzies'll really get down to doing something in space – and that he's likely to be in the forefront of whatever they do do.'

Venus

'And getting a medal for turning us in for piracy won't do him any official harm, either,' added one of the others, bitterly.

'No,' Troon agreed, 'but if the thought of the charge is worrying you, I shouldn't let it. They'll have to put us on trial, of course, but luckily there's been no bloodshed, so the odds are they'll pardon us, or just give us a token penalty. After all, we did get there; and we were the first to make it. Now that we are no longer a danger, sentiment will swing round. They'd lose a devil of a lot of public favour if they tried to keep us in jail for it.'

'Well, that's something – and I reckon you're right,' Arthur admitted. 'Most of the worrying is going to come the way of that organizing genius, your Cousin Jayme – and whoever else put up the money. I never did think they'd get much for all they spent to exploit that lousy planet, anyway, but whatever there is there, the Brazzies are going to get it now. Just a bit too clever for one another, your relatives.'

'Maybe,' admitted Troon, 'but I'd not be sure yet. After all, we did ship Jayme one shuttle-load of specimens, remember. His people working on them will have about two years' start of any Brazzy researchers – and that's quite a lot, with old man Gonveia's botanical organization behind it.'

'All right. Your Cousin Jayme may be a marvel, commercially,' Arthur conceded, 'but your Cousin Jorge has certainly taken him and all of us for a ride, strategically. And thanks to him, damn it, the Brazzies have now got the lot – our ship, our Dome and supplies, all our research work, and us. As profitable a bit of double-crossing as ever there was – with laurels and promotion for Jorge Trunho.'

'Look here,' put in one of the others, 'the Troon family, as everyone knows, has a deserved reputation for gambling

The Outward Urge

with space in a big way. Some of their gambles have come off, and some of them haven't. The first half of this one did, and the second half hasn't. Now I suggest that we agree to drop the subject. We've a long journey ahead, and chawing the subject over and over isn't going to sweeten it, or get us anywhere. Agreed?'

The journey was tedious indeed. Nothing broke it but the regular arrival of meals – covered cans floated into the compartment by one member of the Brazilian Space Force, while another guarded the door. The captives received no bearings, no progress reports, they simply waited timelessly for it to end.

At last it did. For the first time during the trip a concealed speaker broke silence with a click and a scratch.

'Secure all loose objects,' it instructed twice in Portuguese.

The crew of the *Aphrodite* stared at one another, scarcely able to believe that the imprisonment was coming to an end at last. Half an hour later the voice spoke again:

'All loose objects should have been made fast by now. Everyone to couches, and make ready. All to couches; fasten all straps. Deceleration will begin in ten minutes from now.'

Troon opened a port-cover. The slow turn gave him a view of a huge Earth crescent sliding smoothly up the black sky. He secured the cover again, and got on to his couch.

'Not an Earth landing,' he said. 'Must be putting in at Primeira.'

'Four minutes,' announced the loudspeaker.

Primeira, thought Troon, the old threshold of space. I wonder what its builders would have to say if they could see the first successful Venus expedition coming in as prisoners . . . ?

The speaker was counting now. He composed himself to wait for the thrust and the onset of weight.

Venus

One after another Troon's crew jetted themselves across from the *Santa Maria* to Primeira. Once through the airlock there, they took off their space-suits and waited, with a guard in charge of them. During the considerable delay they sat watching other men entering the airlock to go outside. There seemed to be a great many of them. More than an hour passed before the Capitão Camarello and his second-in-command, Jorge Trunho, arrived, and removed their space-suits to reveal themselves dressed in immaculate uniforms for the occasion. It was evident that the handing over of their prisoners to the Commander of the Satellite was to be a formal affair. Troon was not much impressed; he smiled, and tried to catch his cousin's eye; Jorge caught it stonily once, and thereafter avoided it.

Two more armed guards appeared. The party was marched to the Satellite Commander's cabin, and lined up in two ranks. After that, there appeared to be a hitch. For five minutes they waited in silence, then Camarello spoke to Trunho who went back to the door to inquire. They waited another five minutes, then the inner door of the room opened, and a voice said, in English:

'My apologies for keeping you waiting, gentlemen.'

And into the cabin, dressed in an ordinary suit, stepped Jayme Gonveia.

He nodded to Troon.

'Glad to see you, George. I trust you didn't have too uncomfortable a trip.'

'But how did you do it?' Troon wanted to know, later on, when they were alone together.

'Less difficult than you might think,' Jayme told him. 'We put parties aboard the two mothballed Satellites six months ago, and prepared them for action which we hoped would not be necessary. We infiltrated undercover groups

165

both here and on the Moon Station. The rest was mostly a matter of suitable timing.

'I made a mistake over Jorge, though. Perhaps I did not tell him enough. If he had had a better idea of the scale he'd very likely have played straight with us. However, its only effect was to delay the next phase of the operation; we did not want an alarm raised for fear the *Santa Maria* should be diverted, and we need her intact.

'The radio operators were the key men in the takeover. A week ago, the one here, on Primeira, put over the internal speaker system a message announcing that the Moon Garrison had mutinied, imprisoned its officers, and called upon the Primeira crew to do the same. The moon operator put over a similar message, transposing the places. Both of them put their radios temporarily out of action, for safety, but continued to announce previously concocted messages over the internal system. During this stage, small shuttle-type rockets that we have been holding at the other Satellites appeared close to Primeira, and one landed close to the Moon Station.

'Well, as you know, the Space Force was shot through with disaffection. Our undercover groups had worked on the men, and not found it very difficult. They were organized and ready, and were able to take over with very little trouble. Those who wouldn't join us have been transported to one of the mothball Satellites *pro tem*. The only thing that had gone wrong was at your end. The *Santa Maria* was on the way back here. If we made an announcement she would be diverted; in which case we should lose not only your valuable selves, but a very valuable ship. So we made no announcement. We reopened radio communications with excuses about electrical interference, and resumed routine messages as though nothing had happened. We have been bluffing for a week while we waited for you and the *Santa Maria* – and during that time we have acquired a couple of shuttles of provisions as well.

'But in an hour or so now, the news will be broadcast. Camarello and our cousin Jorge have gone over to join the rest of the unpersuadables on the minor Satellite where they will remain until their government sends a ship to fetch them. The exact date and time for that will depend on how long it takes to sink into the official Rio minds that Space is no longer a Province of Brazil.'

Troon thought the position over silently for some moments, then he said:

'I had no idea you were brewing anything on such a scale as this, Jayme.'

'Perhaps I should apologize to you for that, George, but it seemed wise to keep the compartments of the plan separate, as far as possible. And I think it was – it spared you the necessity of acting, and the need to watch yourself for slips.'

'But now the operation is complete, and you are all set to spring it on them that space has become a State of Australia – '

'A State of Australia!' exclaimed Jayme. 'Good God, man, do you think I want to start a war between Brazil and Australia? Certainly not! Space will declare itself an independent territory – if the use of the word "territory" is valid in the circumstances.'

Troon stared at him.

'Independent! For heaven's sake, Jayme, space is – well, I mean, out here, in nothing, like this. I never – why, it's utterly impossible, Jayme!'

Jayme Gonveia smiled gently, and shook his head.

'On the contrary, George. If you will consider the original *raison d'être* of the Satellites and the Moon Station, I think you will see that space, as an entity, is in an excellent position to propose terms. One day it may be in a position to do a useful trade, but until then, it can at least be the policeman of the world – and a policeman is worthy of his hire.'

George Troon continued to gaze reflectively at the floor for a full minute. When he looked up, his expression had lost its incredulity. He did not speak, but Jayme Gonveia replied as if he had.

'Yes, George,' he said. 'From today, your gnat-voices are just a little closer.'

FIVE

THE EMPTINESS OF SPACE:

THE ASTEROIDS A.D. 2194

MY first visit to New Caledonia was in the summer of 2199. At that time an exploration party under the leadership of Gilbert Troon was cautiously pushing its way up the less radio-active parts of Italy, investigating the prospects of reclamation. My firm felt that there might be a popular book in it, and assigned me to put the proposition to Gilbert. When I arrived, however, it was to find that he had been delayed, and was now expected a week later. I was not at all displeased. A few days of comfortable laziness on a Pacific island, all paid for and counting as work, is the kind of perquisite I like.

New Caledonia is a fascinating spot, and well worth the trouble of getting a landing permit – if you can get one. It has more of the past – and more of the future, too, for that matter – than any other place, and somehow it manages to keep them almost separate.

At one time the island, and the group, were, in spite of the name, a French colony. But in 2044, with the eclipse of Europe in the Great Northern War, it found itself, like other ex-colonies dotted all about the world, suddenly thrown upon its own resources. While most mainland colonies hurried to make treaties with their nearest powerful neighbours, many islands such as New Caledonia had little to offer and not much to fear, and so let things drift.

For two generations the surviving nations were far too occupied by the tasks of bringing equilibrium to a half-wrecked world to take any interest in scattered islands. It was not until the Brazilians began to see Australia as a possible challenger of their supremacy that they started a policy of unobtrusive, and tactfully mercantile, expansion into the Pacific. Then, naturally, it occurred to the Australians, too, that it was time to begin to extend *their* economic influence over various island-groups.

The New Caledonians resisted infiltration. They had found independence congenial, and steadily rebuffed temptations by both parties. The year 2144, in which Space declared for independence, found them still resisting; but the pressure was now considerable. They had watched one group of islands after another succumb to trade preferences, and thereafter virtually slide back to colonial status, and they now found it difficult to doubt that before long the same would happen to themselves when, whatever the form of words, they should be annexed – most likely by the Australians in order to forestall the establishment of a Brazilian base there, within a thousand miles of the coast.

It was into this situation that Jayme Gonveia, speaking for Space, stepped in 2150 with a suggestion of his own. He offered the New Caledonians guaranteed independence of either big Power, a considerable quantity of cash, and a prosperous future if they would grant Space a lease of territory which would become its Earth headquarters and main terminus.

The proposition was not altogether to the New Caledonian taste, but it was better than the alternatives. They accepted, and the construction of the Spaceyards was begun.

Since then the island has lived in a curious symbiosis. In the north are the rocket landing and dispatch stages, warehouses and engineering shops, and a way of life furnished with all modern techniques, while the other four-fifths of the island all but ignores it, and contentedly lives much as it did two and a half centuries ago. Such a state of affairs

The Emptiness of Space

cannot be preserved by accident in this world. It is the result of careful contrivance both by the New Caledonians who like it that way, and by Space which dislikes outsiders taking too close an interest in its affairs. So, for permission to land anywhere in the group, one needs hard-won visas from both authorities. The result is no exploitation by tourists or salesmen, and a scarcity of strangers.

However, there I was, with an unexpected week of leisure to put in, and no reason why I should spend it in Space-Concession territory. One of the secretaries suggested Lahua, down in the south at no great distance from Noumea, the capital, as a restful spot, so thither I went.

Lahua has picture-book charm. It is a small fishing town, half-tropical, half-French. On its wide white beach there are still canoes, working canoes, as well as modern. At one end of the curve a mole gives shelter for a small anchorage, and there the palms that fringe the rest of the shore stop to make room for a town.

Many of Lahua's houses are improved-traditional, still thatched with palm, but its heart is a cobbled rectangle surrounded by entirely untropical houses, known as the Grande Place. Here are shops, pavement cafés, stalls of fruit under bright striped awnings guarded by Gauguinesque women, a state of Bougainville, an atrociously ugly church on the east side, a *pissoir*, and even a *mairie*. The whole thing might have been imported complete from early twentieth-century France, except for the inhabitants – but even they, some in bright sarongs, some in European clothes, must have looked much the same when France ruled there.

I found it difficult to believe that they are real people living real lives. For the first day I was constantly accompanied by the feeling that an unseen director would suddenly call 'Cut', and it would all come to a stop.

The Outward Urge

On the second morning I was growing more used to it. I bathed, and then with a sense that I was beginning to get the feel of the life, drifted to the *place*, in search of apéritif. I chose a café on the south side where a few trees shaded the tables, and wondered what to order. My usual drinks seemed out of key. A dusky, brightly saronged girl approached. On an impulse, and feeling like a character out of a very old novel I suggested a pernod. She took it as a matter of course.

'*Un pernod? Certainement, monsieur,*' she told me.

I sat there looking across the Square, less busy now that the *déjeuner* hour was close, wondering what Sydney and Rio, Adelaide and São Paulo had gained and lost since they had been the size of Lahua, and doubting the value of the gains. . . .

The pernod arrived. I watched it cloud with water, and sipped it cautiously. An odd drink, scarcely calculated, I felt, to enhance the appetite. As I contemplated it a voice spoke from behind my right shoulder.

'An island product, but from the original recipe,' it said. 'Quite safe, in moderation, I assure you.'

I turned in my chair. The speaker was seated at the next table; a well-built, compact, sandy-haired man, dressed in a spotless white suit, a panama hat with a coloured band, and wearing a neatly trimmed, pointed beard. I guessed his age at about thirty-four though the grey eyes that met my own looked older, more experienced, and troubled.

'A taste that I have not had the opportunity to acquire,' I told him. He nodded.

'You won't find it outside. In some ways we are a museum here, but little the worse, I think, for that.'

'One of the later Muses,' I suggested. 'The Muse of Recent History. And very fascinating, too.'

I became aware that one or two men at tables within

The Emptiness of Space

earshot were paying us – or rather me – some attention; their expressions were not unfriendly, but they showed what seemed to be traces of concern.

'It is – ' my neighbour began to reply, and then broke off, cut short by a rumble in the sky.

I turned to see a slender white spire stabbing up into the blue overhead. Already, by the time the sound reached us, the rocket at its apex was too small to be visible. The man cocked an eye at it.

'Moon-shuttle,' he observed.

'They all sound and look alike to me,' I admitted.

'They wouldn't if you were inside. The acceleration in that shuttle would spread you all over the floor – very thinly,' he said, and then went on: 'We don't often see strangers in Lahua. Perhaps you would care to give me the pleasure of your company for luncheon? My name, by the way, is George.'

I hesitated, and while I did I noticed over his shoulder an elderly man who moved his lips slightly as he gave me what was without doubt an encouraging nod. I decided to take a chance on it.

'That's very kind of you. My name is David – David Myford, from Sydney,' I told him. But he made no amplification regarding himself, so I was left wondering whether George was his forename, or his surname.

I moved to his table, and he lifted a hand to summon the girl.

'Unless you are averse to fish you must try the bouillabaisse – *spécialité de la maison*,' he told me.

I was aware that I had gained the approval of the elderly man, and apparently of some others as well, by joining George. The waitress, too, had an approving air. I wondered vaguely what was going on, and whether I had been let in for the town bore, to protect the rest.

173

The Outward Urge

'From Sydney,' he said reflectively. 'It's a long time since I saw Sydney. I don't suppose I'd know it now.'

'It keeps on growing,' I admitted, 'but Nature would always prevent you from confusing it with anywhere else.'

We went on chatting. The bouillabaisse arrived; and excellent it was. There were hunks of first-class bread, too, cut from those long loaves you see in pictures in old European books. I began to feel, with the help of the local wine, that a lot could be said for the twentieth-century way of living.

In the course of our talk it emerged that George had been a rocket pilot, but was grounded now – not, one would judge, for reasons of health, so I did not inquire further. . . .

The second course was an excellent coupe of fruits I had never heard of, and, overall, iced passion-fruit juice. It was when the coffee came that he said, rather wistfully I thought:

'I had hoped you might be able to help me, Mr Myford, but it now seems to me that you are not a man of faith.'

'Surely everyone has to be very much a man of faith,' I protested. 'For everything a man cannot do for himself he has to have faith in others.'

'True,' he conceded. 'I should have said "spiritual faith". You do not speak as one who is interested in the nature and destiny of his soul – or of anyone else's soul – I fear?'

I felt that I perceived what was coming next. However if he was interested in saving my soul he had at least begun the operation by looking after my bodily needs with a generously good meal.

'When I was young,' I told him, 'I used to worry quite a lot about my soul, but later I decided that that was largely a matter of vanity.'

The Emptiness of Space

'There is also vanity in thinking oneself self-sufficient,' he said.

'Certainly,' I agreed. 'It is chiefly with the conception of the soul as a separate entity that I find myself out of sympathy. For me it is a manifestation of mind which is, in its turn, a product of the brain, modified by the external environment, and influenced more directly by the glands.'

He looked saddened, and shook his head reprovingly.

'You are so wrong – so very wrong. Some are always conscious of their souls, others, like yourself, are unaware of them, but no one knows the true value of his soul as long as he has it. It is not until a man has lost his soul that he understands its value.'

It was not an observation making for easy rejoinder, so I let the silence between us continue. Presently he looked up into the northern sky where the trail of the moon-bound shuttle had long since blown away. With embarrassment I observed two large tears flow from the inner corners of his eyes and trickle down beside his nose. He, however, showed no embarrassment; he simply pulled out a large, white, beautifully laundered handkerchief, and dealt with them.

'I hope you will never learn what a dreadful thing it is to have no soul,' he told me, with a shake of his head. 'It is to hold the emptiness of space in one's heart: to sit by the waters of Babylon for the rest of one's life.'

Lamely I said:

'I'm afraid this is out of my range. I don't understand.'

'Of course you don't. No one understands. But always one keeps on hoping that one day there will come somebody who does understand and can help.'

'But the soul is a manifestation of the self,' I said. 'I don't see how that *can* be lost – it can be changed, perhaps, but not lost.'

'Mine is,' he said, still looking up into the vast blue. 'Lost – adrift somewhere out there. Without it I am a sham. A man who has lost a leg or an arm is still a man, but a man who has lost his soul is nothing – nothing – nothing. ...'

'Perhaps a psychiatrist – ' I started to suggest, uncertainly. That stirred him, and checked the tears.

'Psychiatrist!' he exclaimed scornfully. 'Damned frauds! Even to the word. They may know a bit about minds; but about the psyche! – why they even deny its existence ...!'

There was a pause.

'I wish I could help...' I said, rather vaguely.

'There was a chance. You *might* have been one who could. There's always the chance. ...' he said consolingly, though whether he was consoling himself or me seemed moot. At this point the church clock struck two. My host's mood changed. He got up quite briskly.

'I have to go now,' he told me. 'I wish you had been the one, but it has been a pleasant encounter all the same. I hope you enjoy Lahua.'

I watched him make his way along the *place*. At one stall he paused, selected a peach-like fruit, and bit into it. The woman beamed at him amiably, apparently unconcerned about payment.

The dusky waitress arrived by my table, and stood looking after him.

'*O le pauvre monsieur Georges*,' she said sadly. We watched him climb the church steps, throw away the remnant of his fruit, and remove his hat to enter. '*Il va faire la prière*,' she explained. '*Tous les jours* 'e make pray for 'is soul. In ze morning, in ze afternoon. *C'est si triste*.'

I noticed the bill in her hand. I fear that for a moment I misjudged George, but it had been a good lunch. I reached

The Emptiness of Space

for my notecase. The girl noticed, and shook her head.

'*Non, non, monsieur, non. Vous êtes convive. C'est d'accord. Alors, monsieur Georges* 'e sign bill tomorrow. *S'arrange. C'est okay,*' she insisted, and stuck to it.

The elderly man whom I had noticed before broke in:

'It's all right – quite in order,' he assured me. Then he added: 'Perhaps if you are not in a hurry you would care to take a café-cognac with me?'

There seemed to be a fine open-handedness about Lahua. I accepted, and joined him.

'I'm afraid no one can have briefed you about poor George,' he said.

I admitted this was so. He shook his head in reproof of persons unknown, and added:

'Never mind. All went well. George always has hopes of a stranger, you see: sometimes one has been known to laugh. We don't like that.'

'I'm sorry to hear that,' I told him. 'His state strikes me as very far from funny.'

'It is indeed,' he agreed. 'But he's improving. I doubt whether he knows it himself, but he is. A year ago he would often weep quietly through the whole *déjeuner*. Rather depressing until one got used to it.'

'He lives here in Lahua, then?' I asked.

'He exists. He spends most of his time in the church. For the rest he wanders round. He sleeps at that big white house up on the hill. His grand-daughter's place. She sees that he's decently turned out, and pays the bills for whatever he fancies down here.'

I thought I must have misheard.

'His grand-daughter!' I exclaimed. 'But he's a young man. He can't be much over thirty....'

He looked at me.

'You'll very likely come across him again. Just as well to

know how things stand. Of course it isn't the sort of thing the family likes to publicize, but there's no secret about it.'

The café-cognacs arrived. He added cream to his, and began:

About five years ago (he said), yes, it would be in 2194, young Gerald Troon was taking a ship out to one of the larger asteroids – the one that de Gasparis called Psyche when he spotted it in 1852. The ship was a space-built freighter called the *Celestis*, working from the moon-base. Her crew was five, with not bad accommodation forward. Apart from that and the motor-section these ships are not much more than one big hold which is very often empty on the outward journeys unless it is carrying gear to set up new workings. This time it was empty because the assignment was simply to pick up a load of uranium ore – Psyche is half made of high-yield ore, and all that was necessary was to set going the digging machinery already on the site, and load the stuff in. It seemed simple enough.

But the Asteroid Belt is still a very tricky area, you know. The main bodies and groups are charted, of course – but that only helps you to find them. The place is full of outfliers of all sizes that you couldn't hope to chart, but have to avoid. About the best you can do is to tackle the Belt as near to your objective as possible, reduce speed until you are little more than local orbit velocity, and then edge your way in, going very canny. The trouble is the time it can take to keep on fiddling along that way for thousands – hundreds of thousands, maybe – of miles. Fellows get bored and inattentive, or sick to death of it and start to take chances. I don't know what the answer is. You can bounce radar off the big chunks and hitch that up to a course-deflector to keep you away from them. But the small stuff is just as deadly to a ship, and there's so much of it about

The Emptiness of Space

that if you were to make the course-deflector sensitive enough to react to it you'd have your ship shying off everything the whole time, and getting nowhere. What we want is someone to come up with a kind of repulse mechanism with only a limited range of operation – say, a hundred miles – but no one does. So, as I say, it's tricky. Since they first started to tackle it back in 2150 they've lost half a dozen ships in there and had a dozen more damaged one way or another. Not a nice place at all ... On the other hand, uranium is uranium....

Gerald's a good lad though. He has the authentic Troon yen for space without being much of a chancer; besides, Psyche isn't too far from the inner rim of the orbit – not nearly the approach problem Ceres is, for instance – what's more, he'd done it several times before.

Well, he got into the Belt, and jockeyed and fiddled and niggled his way until he was about three hundred miles out from Psyche and getting ready to come in. Perhaps he'd got a bit careless by then; in any case he'd not be expecting to find anything in orbit around the asteroid. But that's just what he did find – the hard way....

There was a crash which made the whole ship ring round him and his crew as if they were in an enormous bell. It's about the nastiest – and very likely to be the last – sound a spaceman can ever hear. This time, however, their luck was in. It wasn't too bad. They discovered that as they crowded to watch the indicator dials. It was soon evident that nothing vital had been hit, and they were able to release their breath.

Gerald turned over the controls to his First, and he and the engineer, Steve, pulled space-suits out of the locker. When the airlock opened they hitched their safety-lines on to spring hooks, and slid their way aft along the hull on magnetic soles. It was soon clear that the damage was not on the air-lock side, and they worked round the curve of the hull.

One can't say just what they expected to find – probably an embedded hunk of rock, or maybe just a gash in the side of the hold – anyway it was certainly not what they did find, which was half of a small space-ship projecting out of their own hull.

One thing was evident right away – that it had hit with no great force. If it had, it would have gone right through and out the other side, for the hold of a freighter is little more than a single-walled cylinder: there is no need for it to be more, it doesn't have to conserve warmth, or contain air, or resist the friction of an atmosphere, nor does it have to contend with any more gravitational pull than that of the moon; it is only in the living-quarters that there have to be the complexities necessary to sustain life.

Another thing, which was immediately clear, was that this was not the only misadventure that had befallen the small ship. Something had, at some time, sliced off most of its after part, carrying away not only the driving tubes but the mixing-chambers as well, and leaving it hopelessly disabled.

Shuffling round the wreckage to inspect it, Gerald found no entrance. It was thoroughly jammed into the hole it had made, and its airlock must lie forward, somewhere inside the freighter. He sent Steve back for a cutter and for a key that would get them into the hold. While he waited he spoke through his helmet-radio to the operator in the *Celestis*'s living-quarters, and explained the situation. He added:

'Can you raise the Moon-Station just now, Jake? I'd better make a report.'

'Strong and clear, Cap'n,' Jake told him.

The Emptiness of Space

'Good. Tell them to put me on to the Duty Officer, will you.'

He heard Jake open up and call. There was a pause while the waves crossed and re-crossed the millions of miles between them, then a voice:

'Hullo, *Celestis*! Hullo *Celestis*! Moon-Station responding. Go ahead, Jake. Over!'

Gerald waited out the exchange patiently. Radio waves are some of the things that can't be hurried. In due course another voice spoke.

'Hullo, *Celestis*! Moon-Station Duty Officer speaking. Give your location and go ahead.'

'Hullo, Charles. This is Gerald Troon calling from *Celestis* now in orbit about Psyche. Approximately three-twenty miles altitude. I am notifying damage by collision. No harm to personnel. *Not* repeat *not* in danger. Damage appears to be confined to empty hold-section. Cause of damage ...' He went on to give particulars, and concluded: 'I am about to investigate. Will report further. Please keep the link open. Over!'

The engineer returned, floating a self-powered cutter with him on a short safety-cord, and holding the key which would screw back the bolts of the hold's entrance-port. Gerald took the key, placed it in the hole beside the door, and inserted his legs into the two staples that would give him the purchase to wind it.

The moon man's voice came again.

'Hullo, Ticker. Understand no immediate danger. But don't go taking any chances, boy. Can you identify the derelict?'

'Repeat no danger,' Troon told him. 'Plumb lucky. If she'd hit six feet farther forward we'd have had real trouble. I have now opened small door of the hold, and am going in to examine the forepart of the derelict. Will try to identify it.'

The Outward Urge

The cavernous darkness of the hold made it necessary for them to switch on their helmet lights. They could now see the front part of the derelict; it took up about half the space there was. The ship had punched through the wall, turning back the tough alloy in curled petals, as though it had been tinplate. She had come to rest with her nose a bare couple of feet short of the opposite side. The two of them surveyed her for some moments. Steve pointed to a ragged hole, some five or six inches across, about half-way along the embedded section. It had a nasty significance that caused Gerald to nod sombrely.

He shuffled to the ship, and on to its curving side. He found the airlock on the top, as it lay in the *Celestis*, and tried the winding key. He pulled it out again.

'Calling you, Charles,' he said. 'No identifying marks on the derelict. She's not space-built – that is, she could be used in atmosphere. Oldish pattern – well, must be – she's pre the standardization of winding keys, so that takes us back a bit. Maximum external diameter, say, twelve feet. Length unknown – can't say how much after part there was before it was knocked off. She's been holed forward, too. Looks like a small meteorite, about five inches. At speed, I'd say. Just a minute ... Yes, clean through and out, with a pretty small exit hole. Can't open the airlock without making a new key. Quicker to cut our way in. Over!'

He shuffled back, and played his light through the small meteor hole. His helmet prevented him getting his face close enough to see anything but a small part of the opposite wall, with a corresponding hole in it.

'Easiest way is to enlarge this, Steve,' he suggested.

The engineer nodded. He brought his cutter to bear, switched it on and began to carve from the edge of the hole.

'Not much good, Ticker,' came the voice from the moon. 'The bit you gave could apply to any one of four ships.'

The Emptiness of Space

'Patience, dear Charles, while Steve does his bit of fancy-work with the cutter,' Troon told him.

It took twenty minutes to complete the cut through the double hull. Steve switched off, gave a tug with his left hand, and the joined, inner and outer circles of metal floated away.

'*Celestis* calling moon. I am about to go into the derelict, Charles. Keep open,' Troon said.

He bent down, took hold of the sides of the cut, kicked his magnetic soles free of contact, and gave a light pull which took him floating head-first through the hole in the manner of an underwater swimmer. Presently his voice came again, with a different tone:

'I say, Charles, there are three men in here. All in space-suits – old-time space-suits. Two of them are belted on to their bunks. The other one is ... Oh, his leg's gone. The meteorite must have taken it off ... There's a queer – Oh, God, it's his blood frozen into a solid ball ... !'

After a minute or so he went on:

'I've found the log. Can't handle it in these gloves, though. I'll take it aboard, and let you have particulars. The two fellows on the bunks seem to be quite intact – their suits I mean. Their helmets have those curved strip-windows so I can't see much of their faces. Must've – That's odd ... Each of them has a sort of little book attached by a wire to the suit fastener. On the cover it has: "Danger – Perigoso" in red, and, underneath: "Do not remove suit – Read instructions within," repeated in Portuguese. Then: "Hapson Survival System." What would all that mean, Charles? Over!'

While he waited for the reply Gerald clumsily fingered one of the tag-like books and discovered that it opened concertina-wise, a series of small metal plates hinged together printed on one side in English and on the other in Portuguese. The first leaf carried little print, but what there was was striking. It ran 'CAUTION! Do *NOT* open suit until you have read these instruction or you will KILL the wearer.'

When he had got that far the Duty Officer's voice came in again:

'Hullo, Ticker. I've called the Doc. He says do NOT, repeat NOT, touch the two men on any account. Hang on, he's coming to talk to you. He says the Hapson system was scrapped over thirty years ago – He – oh, here he is. . . .'

Another voice came in:

'Ticker? Laysall here. Charles tells me you've found a couple of Hapsons, undamaged. Please confirm, and give circumstances.'

Troon did so. In due course the doctor came back:

'Okay. That sounds fine. Now listen carefully, Ticker. From what you say it's practically certain those two are not dead – yet. They're – well, they're in cold storage. That part of the Hapson system was good. You'll see a kind of boss mounted on the left of the chest. The thing to do in the case of extreme emergency was to slap it good and hard. When you do that it gives a multiple injection. Part of the stuff puts you out. Part of it prevents the building-up in the body of large ice crystals that would damage the tissues. Part of it – oh, well, that'll do later. The point is that it works practically a hundred per cent. You get Nature's own deep-freeze in space. And if there's something to keep off direct radiation from the sun you stay like that until somebody finds you – if anyone ever does. Now I take it that these two have been in the dark of an airless ship which is now in the airless hold of your ship. Is that right?'

'That's so Doc. There are the two small meteorite holes, but they would not get direct beams from there.'

The Emptiness of Space

'Fine. Then keep 'em just like that. Take care they don't get warmed. Don't try anything the instruction-sheet says. The point is that though the success of the Hapson freeze is almost sure, the resuscitation isn't. In fact, it's very dodgy indeed – a poorer than twenty-five-per-cent chance at best. You get lethal crystal formations building up, for one thing. What I suggest is that you try to get 'em back exactly as they are. Our apparatus here will give them the best chance they can have. Can you do that?'

Gerald Troon thought for a moment. Then he said:

'We don't want to waste this trip – and that's what'll happen if we pull the derelict out of our side to leave a hole we can't mend. But if we leave her where she is, plugging the hole, we can at least take on a half-load of ore. And if we pack that well in, it'll help to wedge the derelict in place. So suppose we leave the derelict just as she lies, and the men too, and seal her up to keep the ore out of her. Would that suit?'

'That should be as good as can be done,' the doctor replied. 'But have a look at the two men before you leave them. Make sure they're secure in their bunks. As long as they are kept in space conditions about the only thing likely to harm them is breaking loose under acceleration, and getting damaged.'

'Very well, that's what we'll do. Anyway, we'll not be using any high acceleration the way things are. The other poor fellow shall have a space burial....'

An hour later both Gerald and his companions were back in the *Celestis's* living-quarters, and the First Officer was starting to manoeuvre for the spiral-in to Psyche. The two got out of their space-suits. Gerald pulled the derelict's log from the outside pocket, and took it to his bunk. There he fastened the belt, and opened the book.

The Outward Urge

Five minutes later Steve looked across at him from the opposite bunk, with concern.

'Anything the matter, Cap'n? You're looking a bit queer.'

'I'm feeling a bit queer, Steve. . . . That chap we took out and consigned to space, he was Terence Rice, wasn't he?'

'That's what his disc said,' Steve agreed.

'H'm.' Gerald Troon paused. Then he tapped the book. 'This,' he said, 'is the log of the *Astarte*. She sailed from the Moon-Station 3 January 2149 – forty-five years ago – bound for the Asteroid Belt. There was a crew of three: Captain George Montgomery Troon, engineer Luis Gompez, radio-man Terence Rice. . . .

'So, as the unlucky one was Terence Rice, it follows that one of those two back there must be Gompez, and the other – well, he must be George Montgomery Troon, the one who made the Venus landing in 2144 . . . And, incidentally, my grandfather. . . .'

'Well,' said my companion, 'they got them back all right. Gompez was unlucky, though – at least I suppose you'd call it unlucky – anyway, he didn't come through the resuscitation. George did, of course. . . .

'But there's more to resuscitation than mere revival. There's a degree of physical shock in any case, and when you've been under as long as he had there's plenty of mental shock, too.

'He went under, a youngish man with a young family; he woke up to find himself a great-grandfather; his wife a very old lady who had remarried; his friends gone, or elderly; his two companions in the *Astarte* dead.

'That was bad enough, but worse still was that he knew all about the Hapson System. He knew that when you go into a deep-freeze the whole metabolism comes quickly to a complete stop. You are, by every known definition and test,

The Emptiness of Space

dead.... Corruption cannot set in, of course, but every vital process has stopped; every single feature which we regard as evidence of life has ceased to exist....

'So you are dead....

'So if you believe, as George does, that your psyche, your soul, has independent existence, then it must have left your body when you died.

'And how do you get it back? That's what George wants to know – and that's why he's over there now, praying to be told....'

I leant back in my chair, looking across the *place* at the dark opening of the church door.

'You mean to say that that young man, that George who was here just now, is the very same George Montgomery Troon who made the first landing on Venus, half a century ago?' I said.

'He's the man,' he affirmed.

I shook my head, not for disbelief, but for George's sake.

'What will happen to him?' I asked.

'God knows,' said my neighbour. 'He *is* getting better; he's less distressed than he was. And now he's beginning to show touches of the real Troon obsession to get into space again.

'But what then?... You can't ship a Troon as crew. And you can't have a Captain who might take it into his head to go hunting through Space for his soul....

'Me, I think I'd rather die just once....'

MORE ABOUT PENGUINS

Penguinews, which appears every month, contains details of all the new books issued by Penguins as they are published. From time to time it is supplemented by *Penguins in Print*, which is a complete list of all books published by Penguins which are in print. (There are well over three thousand of these.)

A specimen copy of *Penguinews* will be sent to you free on request, and you can become a subscriber for the price of the postage. For a year's issues (including the complete lists) please send 30p if you live in the United Kingdom, or 60p if you live elsewhere. Just write to Dept EP, Penguin Books Ltd, Harmondsworth, Middlesex, enclosing a cheque or postal order, and your name will be added to the mailing list.

Some other books published by Penguins are described on the following pages.

Note: *Penguinews* and *Penguins in Print*
are not available in the U.S.A. or Canada

GEORGE ORWELL

NINETEEN EIGHTY-FOUR

1984 is the year in which it happens. The world is divided into three great powers, Oceania, Eurasia, and Eastasia, each perpetually at war with the others. Throughout Oceania 'The Party' rules by the agency of four ministries, whose power is absolute – the Ministry of Peace which deals with war, the Ministry of Love (headquarters of the dreaded Thought Police) which deals with law and order, the Ministry of Plenty which deals in scarcities, and the Ministry of Truth which deals with propaganda. The authorities keep a check on every action, word, gesture, or thought.

George Orwell's satire has been compared with that of Swift, and in *Nineteen Eighty-Four* the satire is the framework for one of the most moving stories to have been published in this generation – the human story of Winston Smith and his revolt against the Party's rule.

Also available

ANIMAL FARM

BURMESE DAYS

A CLERGYMAN'S DAUGHTER

COMING UP FOR AIR

DOWN AND OUT IN PARIS AND LONDON

HOMAGE TO CATALONIA

INSIDE THE WHALE

KEEP THE ASPIDISTRA FLYING

THE ROAD TO WIGAN PIER

DECLINE OF THE ENGLISH MURDER
AND OTHER ESSAYS

COLLECTED ESSAYS, JOURNALISM AND LETTERS
(*Four Volumes*)

NOT FOR SALE IN THE U.S.A.

JOHN WYNDHAM

THE CHRYSALIDS

A thrilling and realistic account of the world beset by genetic mutations.'Jolly good story, well-conceived community, characters properly up to simple requirements. Better than the *Kraken*, perhaps even than the *Triffids*' – *Observer**

THE DAY OF THE TRIFFIDS

The Day of the Triffids is a fantastic, frightening, but entirely plausible story of the future when the world is dominated by triffids, grotesque and dangerous plants over seven feet tall, originally cultivated for their yield of oil but later becoming a menace to their human directors.†

THE KRAKEN WAKES

The title is taken from a poem by Tennyson, and the book tells of the awakening and rise to power of forces from beneath the surface of the sea.*

THE MIDWICH CUCKOOS

This is the book from which the film *The Village of the Damned* was made.*

THE SEEDS OF TIME

The ten stories making up this book are acknowledged by their author as 'experiments in adapting the SF motif to various styles of short story'. The fascinating variety here does much to explain John Wyndham's success.*

TROUBLE WITH LICHEN

'If even a tenth of science fiction were as good, we should be in clover' – Kingsley Amis in the *Observer**

CONSIDER HER WAYS AND OTHERS*

CHOCKY*

*NOT FOR SALE IN THE U.S.A.

†NOT FOR SALE IN THE U.S.A. OR CANADA